ALPHA SQUAD

BOOT CAMP

LORELEI MOONE

eXplicitTales

CONTENTS

CHAPTER ONE

It started as a rather ordinary day in September. Eric King, who had led the London branch of the New Alliance, found himself with not much else to do but to flip through TV channels at home. Ever since the big reveal earlier in the year, the New Alliance had been struggling to remain relevant, and the only real work that had come along was PR related. That was not something Eric was good at.

He—like most bears—was more comfortable outside of the limelight.

So he found himself alone on the sofa, watching the news, which had grown increasingly unnerving over the last few weeks. They kept repeating the same images of seemingly ordinary people—shifters just like him— pouring into makeshift camps in Dover. His heart grew heavy at the sight.

They had done this. The New Alliance, under Henry's leadership, had orchestrated the events that had led up to this mess.

They were lucky with how things had gone down in the UK; the human government seemed to be willing to accept the shifters as part of their citizenry.

But not every country had followed the same approach. That was the reason so many of their kind were now trying to relocate.

France had implemented a mandatory registration policy for all shifters, and The Netherlands had a similar law up for vote in an upcoming referendum. People—humans and shifters alike—were scared of what the future would bring.

The camera panned across the latest group of arrivals: a family of five, scanning their surroundings as they disembarked the ferry that had brought them across the Channel. The children seemed to not realize why they had come across; it was still all a big adventure for them. But the mother's face couldn't disguise the uncertainty she must be feeling.

In her eyes, Eric saw his very own mother, when an unfortunate and badly timed shift on his part had forced them to abandon their hometown of York and find refuge in London when he was only thirteen.

Looking at him and his younger brother now, nobody would be able to guess that they weren't native to Greenwich, East London, where they'd moved to at that time. They'd adopted the local culture flawlessly, down to the right accent and the same dress sense everyone in their age group seemed to follow. They'd done everything they could to avoid standing out.

But it had taken him a long time indeed to feel like he *belonged.* Current events had reminded him of that old struggle.

How long would it take these families? These children?

Some of them had traveled in groups, others had arrived on their own. How long before they could live in peace like they had done before the New Alliance had blown the rules of secrecy to smithereens and exposed all of their kind to the world?

Just because the current government was determined to make shifter equality work didn't mean that their futures were set. It wouldn't take all that much to sway public opinion, perhaps just a few unfortunate events involving shifters, capitalized on by the growing anti-shifter movement under Victor Domnall's leadership. Then, the next general election could turn their reality on its head all over again.

He took a deep breath. It was too late to second-guess their campaign now. No matter how he felt about all this in retrospect, he couldn't take it back.

Even without his involvement, Henry and his people would have just found someone else to run things in London.

His phone rang, forcing him to look away from the depressing images on the TV. He grabbed the remote and muted it.

Speak of the devil, Eric thought as he picked up his phone.

"Henry. What can I do for you?" he answered.

"Eric. I have a job for you," Henry said. There were other hushed voices on the other end of the line, but Eric couldn't make out what was being said.

"What's that?" Eric closed his eyes and pinched the bridge of his nose. He was in too deep. No matter what he thought about the fallout from their campaign, he couldn't back out. All he could do now was help with damage control.

"I would like for you to join Alpha Squad." The line went quiet, as though everyone else on the other end was waiting for Eric's response with bated breaths.

Eric opened his eyes again. The news had switched over to a newsreader in a studio.

Alpha Squad? Him? He wasn't sure how to respond. If that was what Henry wanted, then he ought to agree.

"The training starts Monday," Henry added.

"I thought that was just a PR stunt set up by that politician we met together, Oliver Teese."

"Be that as it may, I think it is vital for us to have one of our own inside the team, don't you think?" Henry said.

Eric made a face. He hated that Henry was right.

"True. All right, as you wish. I'll do it."

Again, a muffled voice said something on the other end of the line, but Eric couldn't identify the exact words.

"Oh, Gail is wondering if your brother might be interested. We need all the help we can get."

Eric sighed. Adam had a bit of a reputation as a troublemaker; at twenty-six, he'd never even held down a regular job.

"Send me the details. I'll talk to him," Eric mumbled.

"Thanks. Knew I could count on your support." With those last words, the line went dead.

Eric sat back and switched the sound of the TV back on when he saw a familiar face appear in the studio: Oliver Teese, the politician.

"So your new position as Secretary for Shifter Affairs is completely unheard of even internationally. How do you intend to put voters' minds at ease about these new developments we've been seeing?" The female reporter turned to Oliver Teese and folded her hands.

"Well, I've said so from the start and will say so again. Shifters do not pose a threat to the general public. I've had the privilege of meeting with them from the start of all this."

"Do you mean you were aware of the New Alliance before they made their presence public?" the reporter said.

The politician smiled mysteriously and waved away her question. His demeanor made the hair on the back of Eric's neck stand upright. *A liar by omission.* "The important thing to remember is that we have the matter under control. We have a reputation internationally as a tolerant, accepting nation, and that's not about to change. Of course, as part of the European Union, citizens of the other member states have the right of free movement, which isn't something we are looking to limit or take away for shifters looking to move here."

The reporter turned to face the camera. "Of course,

freedom of movement applies to all citizens of the Union." She turned back to face Oliver Teese.

"That's right. But it's important for everyone to understand that we are not giving preferential treatment either. Anyone who comes here under the freedom of movement directive will be required to conform to the requirements laid out within."

"Meaning European migrants have to have the means to sustain themselves while they are here?" the reporter asked.

"Indeed. New residents will be required to show proof of income or sufficient capital if they are to stay here permanently or be actively seeking work."

"What about the allegations by Victor Domnall and his group that this influx of shifters is going to swing the balance in their favor as they start to outnumber the human population?"

Oliver Teese let out a chuckle. "I would advise people not to follow that man's sensationalist and outlandish rhetoric. The numbers we are talking about here are tiny in comparison to the human population of this country. There is absolutely no risk of shifters outnumbering humans. Latest data from Dover shows that the shifter migrants coming in have added up to about a thousand at the most over the past three months."

"Right. So compared with normal immigration rates—" the reporter started.

"Compared to normal figures, it's practically

negligible," Oliver Teese interrupted.

"Well, there you have it. That's all we have time for now. Thank you for coming in, Mr. Secretary. Now we go back to Rachel Kinley, in the field in Dover."

Eric picked up the remote and switched off the TV. This whole situation had made the man's career. Hardly anyone had even heard of Oliver Teese before any of this had happened. Eric had only made an appointment for Henry and the team to meet with his office because he was his local Member of Parliament at the time. Not that you could tell as much from looking at him now. He seemed to have received media training during the months leading up to his promotion and was now as smooth and slippery as they came.

Eric shook his head. *Once a politician…*

He picked up his phone and dialed Adam's number. It was noon, still a bit early in the day for his baby brother, but he was keen to get this particular conversation out of the way. Chances were Adam would tell Eric where to shove the suggestion of joining Alpha Squad together, but after getting this over with, at least he could tell Henry that he'd tried.

That was all anyone could expect.

———◆———

Eric was up bright and early on Sunday. Not that it was a must; the drive to Wales, where the training for Alpha

Squad was to take place, was not that long. No, something else had awoken him. Nerves? Doubts about whether he was doing the right thing?

Surprisingly, Adam had agreed to join the taskforce with him. Perhaps it was the promise of a regular paycheck that had attracted him, or perhaps he thought it was glamorous somehow. Either way, he would be arriving sometime during the morning and they'd make the drive up to South Wales together.

The training would be tough. Eric already knew that and was prepared for it. Was Adam? Only time would tell.

He checked his bags for the tenth time, then put the coffee maker on for some much-needed caffeine. A knock on the door of his flat interrupted him.

"Adam." Eric greeted his brother with a quick hug and slap on the back.

"Hey, bro. You ready?" Adam smiled widely. He looked excited.

That was sure to change once he figured out there'd be actual hard work involved in completing the training.

Eric shrugged. "I was just making a coffee. Want some?"

Adam nodded and placed his large gym bag on the ground beside the door before following Eric into the kitchen.

They drank the first cup in silence, with Eric eyeing his younger brother suspiciously. What was going on in Adam's head to make him so cheerful this early on a

Sunday morning? He'd always been the rebellious sort and terrible at accepting authority. That was why Eric hadn't involved him in any New Alliance stuff before the big reveal.

"It'll take us about four hours to get there," Eric said as he poured the remaining coffee into a steel flask.

"Right. Road trip!" Adam cheered.

Eric scrutinized him. Adam was so young when their family moved to the city, he had never had a taste of the great outdoors. The training grounds where they were headed were used by the SAS, among other branches of the armed forces. As bears, they'd have a natural advantage as far as physical training was concerned, but still.

Eric shook his head. He'd figure it out soon enough. Adam wouldn't last more than a few days. A week, at the most.

"Let's go then," Eric said. "The sooner we reach there, the more time we'll have to explore the place before training starts in the morning."

Adam nodded eagerly and grabbed the flask off the counter on his way out, leaving Eric to shake his head some more. This was going to be interesting.

CHAPTER TWO

This assignment was going to be difficult.

Janine looked at herself in the mirror, making sure none of her curled locks had escaped the grasp of the tight bun she usually sported while on duty. She took a deep breath.

Difficult was an understatement. This assignment was crap. It was no wonder none of the boys in her unit had wanted it. So it had been handed to her. A *promotion*, her superiors had said. It really wasn't.

The so-called shifters she was meant to train were not just highly unqualified, they were potentially dangerous. Much stronger than regular people, which would no doubt make them difficult to control. Who knew how they would react to a woman in charge.

And then there were the humans. She wasn't quite sure who her team would comprise of, but the few files she'd been given with her orders did not fill her with confidence. She might struggle to control the human part of the squad as much as the shifters.

But Janine wasn't a quitter. She would give it her all. Failure was not an option.

A quick glance at the clock above her dresser revealed that it was time to leave. She'd drive straight to the base, which would be her new home for the foreseeable future.

Well, hers, and Alpha Squad's—a ridiculously macho name if you asked her. Of course, nobody had asked her.

All her belongings were already stashed in the trunk of her car. The room looked sparse as a result. A blank slate.

It would be a while before she'd come back here. She didn't mind; growing up a foster child, bouncing from home to home, had taught her that nothing in life was permanent. Home was where her work took her. Right now, on this quiet Sunday morning in September, it would take her up the M4 into Wales.

Next? Who knew? One step at a time.

She picked up her appointment letter on the way out.

———◆———

It was about an hour later when Janine pulled into a rest stop. She was only partially motivated by a yearning for caffeine; mostly, it was procrastination that had sparked her decision to take a break.

Motorway service stations were funny places. They weren't destinations, merely stops on the way to somewhere more exciting. By their very nature they felt impermanent.

Even though the summer was now over, some mostly elderly holidaymakers were still on the move, with their overloaded cars and unapologetically informal fashion sense. Janine, despite dressing in civilian clothes today, still stood out as too proper and straight-laced.

"How can I help?" The girl at the hot drinks counter could not have sounded more disinterested if she tried.

"A regular coffee, milk," Janine said. "No, wait, I'll have a cappuccino."

Janine was headed to a remote and only occasionally used army base. Who knew how long it would take to see some semblance of civilization. She might as well treat herself now.

The girl waited for a couple of seconds with a blank look on her face, as though she was expecting Janine to change her mind again, then pressed a few buttons on the till.

"That'll be 4.25." She tapped her fingers impatiently on the counter as Janine retrieved a £5 note from her wallet and handed it to her.

With these prices, it was no wonder that nobody ever came to these places unless they had no other choice.

The girl quickly counted out the change and hurriedly deposited it in Janine's outstretched hand, causing one of the coins to fall onto the ground.

Janine turned to chase after the stray coin only to find it had come to halt against another customer's shoe. A very large, black boot belonging, in fact, as she figured out upon looking up, to a very tall, incredibly broad, and muscular man, who looked down at her with surprisingly warm brown eyes.

"You dropped something," he remarked.

Thanks, yeah, I'd noticed, Janine thought.

Despite the obviousness of his comment, the bass in his voice still managed to send shivers down her spine.

Janine averted her gaze as he bent down and picked up the coin, holding it up in her direction.

"Thanks," she stammered.

Janine took a deep breath, straightened her back, and forced herself to make eye contact again. "Thank you," she repeated herself, this time in a firmer voice.

How did she expect to train a bunch of renegade shifters and humans if she couldn't even interact with one random guy at a motorway service station properly? What the hell had gotten into her?

"You're welcome," the stranger responded, a warm smile on his face.

She returned his smile briefly.

"Your coffee," the irritating girl called out from behind the counter, prompting Janine to turn her back to the ridiculously handsome stranger. In a strange way, it was a relief not to be faced with him anymore, even if it was just for a second.

She nodded curtly at the girl as she took the takeaway cup and a napkin from the tray on the counter, leaving the sachets of sugar behind. She took a sip right away, savoring the taste as well as the sensation of having the soft frothy milk gently touch her lip. She was stalling, obviously, but when she turned around to leave, she found that the man hadn't moved at all and their eyes met again.

Had he been looking at her the whole time?

She nodded at him and made it a point to check her watch on her way past, but his gaze never wavered and she could feel his eyes on her even as she walked away. Rather than taking a seat inside the building to leisurely enjoy her coffee, she walked back to her car.

Ridiculous .

Her career in the army had meant that she had been around plenty of men at the peak of physical fitness before. None had ever affected her so. In fact, she'd found that most guys who hit the gym as much as this guy must have had nothing much going on upstairs. Something in this man's eyes had suggested otherwise. In an exchange that had lasted only a couple of words, she thought she'd seen some hidden depths that suggested he was different somehow.

That didn't make any sense, did it?

Janine placed her coffee in the cup holder underneath the dash and rested her head in her hands. This was all just a stupid diversion. Starting tomorrow, she'd have a difficult job to do, and she couldn't afford the distraction.

A knock on the window brought her back to reality.

Sure enough, she looked up to find the same guy smiling down at her.

She reluctantly opened her window. *Bloody hell, now what?*

"You were in such a rush, you forgot this inside." He raised his arm to reveal Janine's handbag hanging from his index finger.

"Oh my God," Janine blurted out as he handed it to her. "I don't know where my head is at today."

His smile grew. "Glad to be of service," he said.

This moment was going from bad to worse. In trying to avoid any more awkwardness, she had managed to further embarrass herself.

"Well, thanks again," she said.

The man continued to look down at her for a couple of seconds too long, like he was about to say something else.

"Hey, bro," another guy interrupted. "I'd been looking for you everywhere. Wanna get some lunch?"

The two looked eerily similar, roughly the same height and equally built. Their similarities continued in hair color as well as facial features. Clearly they actually *were* brothers. Funnily, looking at the other one didn't affect her nearly as much, though.

"I'd best be on my way," she mumbled as she zipped up her handbag and placed it upright in the center of the passenger seat.

"Me too." The stranger shot her a last warm smile and nodded his goodbye.

Janine breathed a sigh of relief when he turned around and walked back toward the restaurant. It was only once they'd gone inside that she mustered the will to turn the key.

That was awkward. *It's for the best if I never see that guy again,* Janine told herself. Only part of her believed it; her chest felt heavy with disappointment.

Her job had meant she'd had to forego things other women her age had taken for granted: relationships, the idea of starting a family. She'd always put her work first and today was no different. Usually she never minded, because she felt she was making a difference with her life, but today, that wasn't quite the case. Today, part of her felt like she was heading for disaster with an assignment that was doomed from the start.

She turned on the stereo and increased the volume as her favorite CD started to play. No matter what the outcome, she still had a job to do, and she'd better not be late for it.

General Stone would already be on base, waiting to brief her upon her arrival. Before long, she'd find out exactly how doomed her career was.

With renewed resolve, she took one last sip of coffee before pulling out of the service station. Janine didn't stop again until she reached General Stone's office in the center of the grounds belonging to the Infantry Battle School in Brecon. It was a well-established base that had been in regular use since the start of the Second World War. And General Stone, as its highest-ranking officer, had a reputation that extended well beyond its boundaries.

She was as ready as ever as she stepped inside and reported for duty.

"At ease, Major. Have a seat." The general barely

looked at her while she sat down in the chair in front of his spotlessly clean desk. He continued to sift through the file in front of him, making her wait for another few minutes, when he finally sat back in his leather chair and folded his hands.

"Major, we must discuss Alpha Squad," he began.

Janine nodded. "Yes, sir."

"What do you know of its history, however short?"

"Sir, Alpha Squad was envisioned by the Secretary for Shifter Affairs to help other law enforcement agencies manage shifter related incidents."

The general nodded gravely, then leaned forward. "The Secretary of Shifter Affairs, yes. In your opinion—and you may speak freely—is it the place of the Ministry of Shifter Affairs to set up law enforcement squads such as this?"

Janine blinked a few times. She did not like where this was going. Whether she could speak freely or not was hardly the point. "Sir, it is not my place to decide that. Orders are orders." Plus, technically Parliament had set up Alpha Squad, after the Ministry simply advised there was a need for such a unit.

"I'm glad to hear you say that. Orders are orders, indeed. Since you are a major in the British Army, you are bound by orders that follow the proper chain of command."

"Yes, sir," Janine confirmed. So the plot thickened. She shouldn't have been surprised that the general did not approve of the new task force. But he was being so obvious about it…

"Glad you agree. So I can count on your loyalty to the uniform and the chain of command then?"

Janine nodded. "Yes, sir. Absolutely, sir."

"The Ministry of Shifter Affairs is making a lot of headlines lately. We don't want to rock the boat, so, outwardly it must seem like Alpha Squad has been given a chance. But it must not interfere with the traditional order of affairs. It shall not succeed, do you understand me?"

"I understand, Sir," Janine confirmed.

"Wonderful. Your loyalty will be rewarded once all of this has passed. Now, Alpha Squad has been assigned a barracks on a disused part of the base; as you might understand, we hope to keep your unit away from the regular Infantry recruits as much as possible."

Janine nodded. Fair enough. That might give her enough space to conduct her training as she saw fit. "Yes, Sir."

"You are dismissed, Major Williams." The general picked up the phone from the corner of his desk and started to dial a number, signaling it was time for Janine to leave his office.

What the hell had she gotten herself into?

CHAPTER THREE

Eric and Adam pulled into the base early in the afternoon. It had taken longer than predicted, mainly because the directions hadn't been as straightforward as Eric had assumed before setting off; Google Maps clearly didn't know everything.

The other, perhaps even more significant reason was lunch. Eric's encounter with the mystery woman at the motorway services had been a huge distraction. What was it about her that had affected him so?

After their break, he'd made Adam drive and spent the entire rest of the way reliving his short encounter with her. She was so different from any of the women he'd been with before. The way she carried herself: proud and confident, right until the moment they spoke. Her polished and very proper exterior hid a vulnerable, gentler side which she seemed uncomfortable with. She was not the sort of woman who liked to show weakness.

"That must be it." Adam pointed at the square concrete building at the end of the scruffy looking asphalt track they'd followed for the last couple of miles. Adam parked between an old army green Land Rover, which looked like it had been here forever, and a couple of more modern sedans. Adam was right, this had to be the place. And at least they weren't the first ones here.

They both got out and looked around. Although Adam and Eric were city shifters, their instincts still guided a lot of what they did; surveilling their surroundings before entering a new place was simply routine for them.

Although the larger training area they found themselves on was a proper training establishment which was buzzing with activity, this particular part, with its run-down hangar, overgrown barracks, and discarded old equipment and vehicles, seemed to be mostly disused.

The perfect home for a task force that from its inception was never meant to be relevant in any way. Eric sighed.

"This place looks mental," Adam remarked.

Eric shrugged. "I can't say I'm surprised."

"Do you see that?" Adam pointed at an old tank, which had seemingly been abandoned in the middle of a field. "Do you think they'll let us drive tanks?"

Eric frowned. Looking at the amount of weeds beside the tank, nature was doing its best to reclaim it for itself. And despite all he saw here, Adam *still* seemed excited. He shook his head. There was nothing he could say to his little brother to convince him of anything. He had to work the reality of their situation out for himself.

"Certainly not *that* one," Eric said.

"I wonder who else is inside." Before Eric could stop him, Adam started marching toward the front door and stepped inside.

He only barely caught up with him indoors.

"Hello?" Adam called out.

They both followed a couple of male voices coming from further inside the building, when they were intercepted by a petite female in uniform. "Mr. King, and, uh, Mr. King, I presume?" she said, checking a list on her clipboard.

"Eric King, yes, this is my brother, Adam," Eric said.

Adam nodded in agreement and stretched out his hand at the woman.

"Private Callahan. Um, if you'll follow me inside, we can get you settled in." The woman stared at Adam's hand for a second, didn't reciprocate the gesture, and abruptly turned around and took the lead down the hall. Adam shrugged and followed her with Eric closely on his heels.

The building was well beyond its prime. A fresh coat of paint, no doubt applied in preparation for Alpha Squad's training here, did not disguise the musty scent of the old walls below. The smell of abandonment clung to the building too staunchly to be scared off by a spot of home improvement.

As they got further inside, the voices they'd heard grew louder.

Private Callahan stopped in front of a door, then turned around and stepped aside. "Your quarters. I'll be in the office by the entrance if you need me."

Before they had the chance to say anything, she had already walked off again. Clearly it was a busy day today, with all the new recruits arriving one after the other.

Eric shrugged and turned the handle. Immediately, the chatter inside stopped. The door opened with a loud creak. Again, the fresh paint did not fool him. This place was old and had until recently been completely unloved.

He stepped inside and was greeted by three pairs of eyes. Two men had occupied a bunk bed to the left of the room, whereas the third sat by himself at the far end.

Human, human, wolf. Eric's nose told him as much.

"Hi there, I'm Eric King, this is my brother, Adam," he introduced himself, approaching the nearest human to his left with an outstretched hand.

The man, who looked to be in his forties, eyed him suspiciously. His controlled body language and trim physique suggested he had some kind of military or police training.

Despite waiting for a couple of seconds too long, a handshake was not forthcoming, so Eric withdrew his hand. Then he glanced up at the younger human male who lounged on the top bunk.

"Ben Cooper, Border Force. The grumpy sod in the bottom bunk is Craig Bentley, Special Forces."

"That's Captain Bentley, to you, Cooper," the other man barked.

Ben Cooper made a gesture, brushing his remark aside. "If you say so, mate. We're all stuck in the same rotten boat together now, though, aren't we?"

Eric nodded, slowly. "In the same boat, indeed," he mumbled as he crossed the dormitory, approaching the only other shifter in the room.

"And you are?" Eric asked.

"Thomas Blackwood." The wolf's eyes darted from the humans back to Eric. "Wolf, from the Rannoch clan."

They shook hands. "Brown bear. New Alliance, London branch," Eric said.

The older of the two humans—Bentley—let out a snort, but didn't speak. Eric shot him a disapproving glance.

"I'm Adam." Eric's brother joined his side in front of the wolf's bunk bed. "Do you know if anyone else is joining us?"

Thomas shrugged. "The team leader isn't even here yet. A Major Williams, from the British Army, or so I've been told."

Eric nodded. "Very well. I suppose we can take that bunk over there, then." He lifted his luggage and set it down on the bottom bed. Adam did the same with the top bunk.

As Eric sat, and finally lowered himself onto the firm mattress, which squeaked under his significant weight almost as much as the door hinges had done, he felt very far away from his regular life. He'd joined only on Henry's urging, and ten minutes into the wretched affair, it already seemed to be a disaster. They were supposed to be a team? The divide between the human and shifter elements were deep; how would they overcome that kind of ingrained suspicion and prejudice?

Eric didn't know much about the armed forces, or even law enforcement, but he did know that in a role like this you had to depend on the person next to you, sometimes trusting them with your life. That was how the old as well as New Alliance had functioned too. He absolutely did not trust the humans, especially Bentley, who hadn't even bothered to greet him and Adam when they came in.

Adam climbed up onto the top bed, making the metal frame groan even louder in protest. *This contraption better hold.*

Eric took a deep breath and closed his eyes. He should have just stayed behind at that service station, perhaps tried to strike up more of a conversation with the mysterious woman who had caught his eye there. Or ideally, he should have risked Henry's disapproval and refused to join the task force. Anything was better than this.

Back to the mystery woman. And what a woman she was. A regal beauty, with a voice that had set his heart alight. His inner bear had tried its best to claw to the surface; he'd hardly been able to control the urge to shift right there in front of her.

How would she have reacted if she'd seen his true form? Things had changed since the New Alliance's little stunt, coming out to the entire world media, but they hadn't changed *that* much for everyone. Humans were still apprehensive, and why wouldn't they be? Most of their kind were pretty damn scary looking.

Would she have screamed and run away? Or would she have been intrigued?

He would never find out of course, because he'd let that opportunity pass him by when Adam had dragged him back to the restaurant for lunch.

Where was she now? And was she thinking about their little encounter as much as he was?

So many questions he'd never get the answer to…

Instead, he was stuck here in this decrepit old building with a bunch of people, none of whom seemed to want to be here. Except Blackwood the wolf, maybe. He had seemed like the most cheerful person here after Adam.

The sound of the door disturbed his gloomy thoughts, but he tried to ignore the intrusion.

"Attention!" Private Callahan's voice filled the dorm.

Eric opened his eyes and sat up straight on his bed. The top of his head almost touched the springs underneath Adam's mattress above.

The private stepped aside and another woman marched into the room.

Was he still daydreaming? He could not believe who had entered—the woman he'd just been fantasizing about.

"Major Williams would like to say a few words," Private Callahan said.

Major Williams. Eric was speechless. He had expected a grey-haired man, gruff like the SAS guy across the room, but perhaps more polished. Their commander was a woman. *His* woman.

Major Williams scanned the room, slowly, pausing on each of the other trainees for a moment, then moving on to the next. Until she spotted Eric. She looked away instantly. Of course, she'd recognized him as well, and she did not look pleased to find him here.

"I am Major Janine Williams, your team leader. Welcome and thank you for joining Alpha Squad. Starting tomorrow, I will conduct your training, evaluate you, and report on the progress of this task force with the relevant higher authorities. The first phase of training starts in the morning and will last two weeks, at the end of which you will all be graded on various aspects of your performance. Anyone who is deemed unfit to continue will be asked to leave at that point, before phase two begins. Any questions?"

Questions? Eric had so many of those. He did not speak, though.

"What do you mean, unfit? I was told I was being transferred here permanently," Ben, the younger of the two humans complained.

"You shall address me as Major Williams or Ma'am, first of all. Secondly, this task force is not a joke. Only those who are worthy will make the cut." The major glared at him from across the room. Eric couldn't help but be impressed by her show of authority.

Cooper folded his arms and pressed his lips together.

"Do you understand? What's your name?"

"Ben Cooper, Ma'am. Yes, I understand."

Eric had trouble suppressing a smile. She wasn't going to take any crap from anyone, that much was obvious. It would only be a matter of time before Adam and the major would clash similarly. Amusingly, he found himself rooting not for his brother, but for the woman. Training under her command could get interesting.

She glanced at him for a split second, during which he did his best to hide his reaction. He would play along, fall in line, and do his best to fit into the squad. He owed it to Henry, but that was not the only reason. Fate had handed him a second chance after he recklessly failed to get her details earlier today. No matter what, Eric was not going to waste the opportunity. He'd prove his worth to her one way or another before training was over.

"All right then, at ease, everyone," the major said, "You have a big day ahead of you and I suggest you take rest."

Eric nodded, mostly to himself, and lay back on his cot again. Perhaps this whole Alpha Squad nonsense had a couple of silver linings after all.

CHAPTER FOUR

Of all the people in the entire country, *he* had to be here. The guy from the service station.

Janine had tried to maintain her composure while she welcomed her new recruits and encouraged them to introduce themselves. But on the inside, she was in turmoil.

Now that she was on her own again in her sparsely furnished office, she could barely contain herself anymore.

Bloody great.

"Can I get you anything, Ma'am?" Private Callahan asked as she stuck her head in the door.

Janine looked up, and in a rare moment of weakness, she waved her assistant into the room for as much of a heart-to-heart as a woman in her position could afford.

"Take a seat, Callahan."

The petite woman hesitated for a moment, then did as she was told. They had come across each other briefly on other assignments, but the two of them had never worked closely together. Certainly not enough to build up any kind of rapport or trust.

"You've been briefed by General Stone?" Janine asked.

"Yes, Major," the private answered.

"And what were his orders to you? Bear in mind I'm your superior on this team…"

The woman blinked a couple of times, as though Janine's question had surprised her. It wasn't normal to ask such candid questions of course, but these were not normal circumstances. If she was going to do this job and do it well, Janine needed to know if she could rely on the private going forward.

"I was told I should support you to the best of my abilities. Whatever you need, Ma'am."

Good answer, one which covered all kinds of potential sins. Although General Stone's briefing with Janine herself had been anything but standard, she still expected him to respect the normal order of things. He would not have told Private Callahan the plan; she was too low on the military food chain to be involved. Plus, the fewer people who knew, the better.

"Permission to speak freely, private. What do you make of our recruits?"

Private Callahan pressed her lips together, her eyes darting skittishly toward the open door.

Janine nodded at her, prompting her to jump up and close the door carefully.

"Ma'am, I have some reservations."

Janine folded her hands and looked down at the various files strewn across her desk. She had reservations herself.

"Specifically?"

"Well, Captain Bentley is used to being in command, so

he might have a learning curve ahead of him."

Janine nodded. "Agreed. Anyone else who stands out?"

"The King brothers, Ma'am…" Private Callahan stared at Janine with wide eyes, presumably while trying to formulate a tactful response.

"The younger one has a history of troublesome behavior. Police were involved a number of times while he was still a juvenile. Nothing we couldn't train out of him, but the older one, Eric…"

"Yes?"

"Again, someone who is used to being in more of a leadership role himself. And he's so big and strong… I have to wonder how well he will do. Their lack of formal law enforcement background is also worrying."

Janine nodded again, ignoring the inappropriate tone the private had used. He *was* huge, there was no denying that. Six and a half feet according to his file, although he looked taller in person. And a bear shifter. She should have guessed when she first came across the man that there was something superhuman going on with him. He was out of this world.

Focus, Janine!

"I suppose we will find out soon enough how well these guys respond to the training, Ma'am."

"Yes we will, starting tomorrow. Thank you, Callahan. Dismissed!" Janine picked up a notepad from the far side of her desk and a pen. As soon as the private had left her office, closing the door behind her again, Janine breathed a sigh of relief.

If she was going to survive this infernal assignment, she had to stay on task. And the first job was to formulate a training schedule for this group of misfits. No matter what General Stone had ordered, she still had to give the impression that she was giving these guys a real shot after all.

Janine started by preparing a standard chart to evaluate the recruits. Beside each name, she added some columns representing traits she would grade each trainee on, including physical and mental aptitude, attitude, and ability to follow orders. When she was done, she put her pen down and stared at the chart. If she graded these men the way she normally would, she did not expect any of them to even pass, never mind perform well on paper.

Whether on purpose or otherwise, General Stone might just get his way automatically. The selection process, or lack thereof, which had resulted in this bunch of recruits, had already ensured as much. Alpha Squad would fail at the first hurdle, it was inevitable.

————— • • —————

"Wake up, cadets!" Janine nodded at Private Callahan to flip the light switch in the dorm room, which revealed all her recruits in various stages of drowsiness.

The first to jump up was the former SAS guy, predictably. They trained tardiness right out of those guys.

Within moments of Janine's initial call, Craig Bentley stood to attention in front of his bed. All the while, the younger man in the top bunk, Ben Cooper, got up on his elbows and blinked against the light.

"What time is it?" he mumbled.

Janine tapped her foot impatiently. "It's time to start your training, that's what time it is!"

The solitary man at the end of the dorm joined Craig Bentley in the center of the room, copying his stance. "Ready, Ma'am."

Janine shook her head as she stole a glance at the two brothers from East London, who seemed to find it most difficult to wake up. Perhaps animal stereotypes applied to shifter people as well. Did bear shifters hibernate like real-life bears did? If the weather turned, perhaps she'd find out first hand.

"I'll meet you all outside in ten minutes. No exceptions!" Janine marched out of the room with Callahan closely on her heels.

"That could have gone better," Janine mumbled.

"It's only the first morning," Callahan responded, in a similarly muted tone.

She was right—it was only the first day—but these guys seemingly had no clue what lay ahead.

Janine still found herself shaking her head as she made her way through the hallway and into her office to pick up her clipboard and stopwatch. She also grabbed a coat from the rack in the corner—mornings in the area could be harsh and unpredictable, and she did not expect to be able to head back indoors for quite some time.

Before long, she and Callahan found themselves out on the rather unimpressive grounds next to the parking lot. She had mentally mapped out a trail for everyone to follow this morning, so that she could get a baseline of their fitness levels. They all looked fit enough, but you could never really tell with new recruits until you put them to the test.

It did not take long for the first of the lot to come out. Unsurprisingly, the SAS man, Bentley, led the way, along with the most unlikely of the lot: Eric King.

Janine held her breath as she looked squarely at the two of them. *Must not show weakness. I am in charge.*

Within minutes, the remaining recruits had made it outside as well, though they did not look happy about waking so early. Janine decided to ignore the sorry state of their uniforms for the moment; that could be addressed another day.

"So kind of you to join me. Let's not waste any more time. We'll start with a run around the compound. From this point over here, follow the track around the old tank toward the tree line beyond the old hangar, around the western side of the fence and back here." Janine raised the stopwatch. "And yes, I will be timing you. On three, Callahan!"

Janine waited as the private counted to three and

pressed the button. What she saw took her breath away.

The former SAS guy started strong, as expected, but the three shifters left him in a cloud of dust within moments of the countdown. It was still dark out, so Janine had trouble focusing on their movements. She could barely even see who was leading the race. One of the pack had made it to the trees and was coming back already, while the other human, Cooper—the youngest of the squad— had only reached halfway.

Janine put a comment on his grade sheet to that effect; there was no need to wait for the end of the race to know that he would be last.

Barely a minute later, the first two recruits stopped in front of Janine, prompting her to record their times. It was Thomas Blackwood and Eric King, with Adam following half a minute later. Unbelievable, how fast these guys were, especially considering their size.

"Very good," Janine mumbled as she watched Bentley approach the ground as well.

He stopped and eyed the shifters darkly. Clearly, he'd come into this thinking that his background would give him an edge over everyone else.

"Good job, Bentley," Janine said, only to be met by a similar displeased look.

She didn't let it bother her. He'd been fast for a human, but when it came to running, even the most highly trained man could not beat a wolf or a bear.

They waited for another couple of minutes until

Cooper finally arrived too, panting heavily as he stopped, resting his hands on his thighs.

"Cooper, you made it," Janine remarked, scribbling his terrible time onto the mark sheet. "I think you should work on your stamina daily from now on. I wouldn't want you to lag behind if we're deployed together."

He looked up and made a face. "I didn't see you run with us. Perhaps I won't be the one lagging."

Janine straightened herself. "We've had this discussion before on how to address me. Seeing as you need to build up your fitness, push-ups will do you good. Let's start with twenty."

Cooper frowned.

"Did you not hear me? Get on the ground right now!"

"It's muddy!" he complained, then looked up at Janine again. "Ma'am."

"That's nothing compared to what's coming. I wasn't asking! Do it or you're off the team!"

He sighed and did as he was told. Someone else snorted in amusement.

"You laugh and you're joining him!" Janine warned.

The resulting silence was deafening.

Janine shook her head and made yet another comment behind Cooper's name. *Serious problem with authority.*

"While Cooper completes his pushups, the rest of you will set up the obstacle course. You know the drill, Bentley, you're in charge!" Janine ordered.

She guided everyone toward the old hangar, all the while trying to locate the correct key in the big bunch that covered the entire training grounds. As soon as she had opened the rusty door, she stood by and watched Bentley take the lead. Finally, the gruff man seemed to be in his element, shouting instructions at the three shifters.

She took note of the man's tone and overall demeanor throughout. This task, as well as putting Bentley in charge of it, was yet another test, of course.

Meanwhile, Cooper joined the group and was instantly put to work by Bentley as well. Callahan had pointed out Bentley and the two bear shifters as the biggest potential liabilities on the team, but as the sun finally rose above the hills surrounding the camp, those three seemed much more comfortable than Cooper. Janine was going to have to take him aside for a word later. His attitude left a lot to be desired.

It was only eleven as she caught herself paying a lot more attention to this odd one out on the team, rather than the rest of them. It seemed she was willing to do anything but to spend too much time scrutinizing Eric for fear of getting distracted. This was something she would have to work on for herself, just not today.

CHAPTER FIVE

The first morning of training had gone well; at least, Eric thought it had. As he found himself sitting around a large wobbly table inside a kitchen cum break room with the remaining recruits, one of them, especially, could not keep quiet.

"That was fun, wasn't it? I wonder what else we're going to end up doing," Thomas Blackwood, the wolf, said.

Eric eyed him across the table in silence, preferring to stay in the background as the conversation unfolded. Blackwood looked even more excited now than Adam had been on their way here.

Bentley didn't hold back as much. "This isn't the scouts, you know. Despite what you lot have been led to believe, this place hasn't always been the joke it is today. Good men have died training on these grounds."

Thomas shrugged. "Don't feel bad just because I beat your time on the obstacle course. In fact, the three of us decimated your time, didn't we, lads?"

Adam grinned. "And that was after setting the thing up while you stood by and watched, ain't that right?"

Eric shrugged. So what, the shifters had ruled the obstacle course. What else was new?

"And how about the major, huh? She's quite

something," Thomas said.

Eric's ears perked up. If he said anything more, anything that could even remotely be construed as disrespectful, he would ignore the whole us vs. them dynamic the shifters and humans had fallen into and take Thomas' head off for it.

"She's our superior. It would serve you well to remember that," Bentley said. His condescending tone did not match his words. He didn't give the impression of ever being impressed by anyone, especially not her.

"Hey, anyone else hungry?" Adam remarked.

All heads, including Eric's, turned in his direction.

"I mean, we've been here almost a day now, and I've still not seen any kitchen staff arrive."

Bentley rested his head in his hands. "You're having a laugh, right?"

Adam glared at the man. "What's your point?"

"Kitchen staff… Where do I begin," Bentley mumbled to himself.

Eric sat back and watched. His little brother could take care of himself; then again, Eric already knew where this was going, whereas Adam still had a lot to learn.

"This ain't a hotel. If you're hungry, you do something about it."

Adam opened his mouth to respond, but then closed it again without saying anything.

"I'm sure the major and that little fox, Callahan, aren't sitting around starving to death," Cooper quipped from his corner of the table.

He and his big mouth still had not learned a thing. No matter, Eric thought to himself. The inevitable extra push-ups his attitude would earn him would do him good. So far he had been the weakest of the group.

"What Major Williams does is none of your concern. We're but lowly cadets. We haven't yet earned the right to be waited on," Bentley grumbled.

"Aight. So. Who's hungry, then?" Adam rephrased his earlier question, in a gruffer tone.

Bentley shrugged and stared straight ahead. Eric and Blackwood nodded, as did Cooper, but nobody made a move.

Finally, Eric gave in and got up to help his brother, who had already started rifling through the refrigerator. There was nothing much inside, just some eggs and bread. The various cupboards were equally bare.

"Finally, something I have valuable previous experience for," Adam grumbled to himself as he started assembling the makings of a very basic meal.

Eric couldn't suppress a chuckle. His brother had never held onto a regular job, but he *had* worked in the kitchen of a local café one summer when he was still in school. He had lasted all of two weeks in that role, before flipping off the owner in a dispute over who was going to do the dishes.

Just as Adam began frying up some eggs, a crackly and

distorted version of Private Callahan's voice interrupted their activities.

"All recruits are requested to report to Major Williams' office one after the other. Work out the order amongst yourselves." Another crackle signaled the end of the announcement.

Eric couldn't help but wonder if the timing of the announcement was deliberate. He scanned all corners of the room, and sure enough, there was a small red light inside a vent beside intercom speaker. A human eye would have never picked it up, but Eric could spot something shiny like a small camera lens in there.

They were being watched. *Obviously.*

Nothing was quite as it seemed in this place.

Adam shrugged as he continued to operate the stove. "One of you lot go first. I'm busy."

The two humans did not seem keen, but Blackwood jumped up. "All right then! Wonder what this is about."

Eric waved him down. "I'll go. You guys eat first."

The wolf shrugged and sank back down onto his chair. "If you prefer."

He did, actually. If this was anything like the basic training he'd undergone with the New Alliance, it was time for individual assessments. Perhaps the major had prepared some tests for each recruit, or she would just wing it and have conversations with each of them.

In any case, he welcomed the chance for some alone time with her, no matter how loudly his stomach growled.

He could not explain it, neither did he expect anything to happen. He just knew that he craved to be near her. His inner bear practically demanded it.

———◆———

"Come in," Janine answered the knock on her door.

Individual assessments were an essential part of training, but she was dreading one in particular this time. Eric King.

Of course it was him who had decided to come in first. She held her breath as she observed him enter her office. His movements were much more stealthy and refined than she would expect from someone of his stature. Was it deliberate?

Either way, hopefully, she could get this conversation out of the way quickly, so that she could move on to the easier subjects.

"Take a seat," she offered.

Cadet King—she'd tried to force herself to think of him in those terms, even if it seemed wholly inappropriate—sat down. He made the substantial wood and leather chair in front of her desk look small underneath him.

Her heartbeat sped up against her will.

His eyes were fixed on her face as he folded his hands and waited for further instructions. Despite Callahan's observations as well as her own concerns, he had been quite comfortable taking orders all morning. Was it just an act?

"I have a few questions for you, and it's best if you are completely honest." Janine shuffled a few of the papers on her desk, pretending to look for the checklist she had prepared earlier. In reality, she was just trying to avoid eye contact.

"Of course, Ma'am."

His voice still affected her, perhaps even more so than the first time they'd spoken. He was so near and yet so unattainable. She could not wait for this torture to be over.

She glanced up into his eyes and immediately focused on the questionnaire again.

"Why are you here?" she started, folding her hands to resist the urge to fidget with the paperwork again.

"You called all of us in," Cadet King—Eric—answered.

Janine shook her head. *Don't make this any more difficult than it has to be!* "I mean generally. Why join Alpha Squad?"

He paused, stealing a glance downward, presumably at her lips. Her heart skipped a few beats, but she did her best to maintain the same steely expression.

You're mine, a voice said in her head. Was it a voice, though? It sounded more like a low growl. Janine readjusted one hand on top of the other and continued to stare straight at the bear of a man in front of her. Now she was truly losing it.

"As you will have read in my file, I've been involved in the New Alliance. I just want to make a difference,

Ma'am."

And what a difference you've made already, Janine thought.

I'm here to claim you, the same voice in her head seemed to say. The hairs on her arms stood upright, tempting her to scratch herself, but she managed to resist the urge. Janine's eye twitched involuntarily. What *was* that voice?

"In your own words: what is the purpose of Alpha Squad? The mission statement, if you will…"

Eric continued to look at her directly, his expression as calm as could be.

"To aid the traditional law enforcement agencies in any shifter related matters."

Janine nodded and made a quick note in his file. "Let's drill down, shall we? In concrete terms, what are we here for?"

"For example, shifter on shifter or shifter on human crime. We could more effectively investigate the shifters in question. We would be a bridge between the shifter community and the human government."

Janine scribbled his response onto a further sheet of paper, rushing so much the end result was hardly legible. Still, if her previous interactions with this man were any indication, she wouldn't need the notes to recall his answers word for word. This conversation would get replayed and analyzed over and over during those moments when she lay in bed at night with sleep still eluding her.

Whether she liked it or not.

"Very good. So would you say you are here because you believe Alpha Squad will continue to let you make a difference?" As soon as Janine finished her question, she listened for his response, as well as any more comments from that weird imaginary voice she'd heard before.

"Yes. Absolutely." That was it. The other voice remained silent.

Janine glanced up at him briefly again. He sounded firm and determined, but there was something in his eyes that suggested that he was either hiding something or not completely convinced of his own answer.

Fair enough, neither was she. He talked the talk, though, and that was all that mattered for now.

She asked him a few more routine questions about his background, how he grew up, his skill set, and what he thought his strengths and weaknesses were, and that concluded the assessment. The mysterious voice seemed to have gone away by itself.

Her phone rang with impeccable timing.

"That's all, then. Excuse me," she said, gesturing at the phone.

Eric, no, Cadet King, nodded and started to get up while she lifted the receiver to her ear.

"Ma'am, the Secretary of Shifter Affairs is on the line for you. He wants an update on the Squad," Callahan explained.

"No problem. Put him through."

Janine watched as Eric left. That had gone pretty well,

hadn't it? She hoped she'd been able to disguise her discomfort well throughout his assessment.

Meanwhile, a voice she'd previously only heard in the media answered the other line. "Major Williams? This is Oliver Teese. You are the officer in charge of Alpha Squad, am I correct?"

"Secretary Teese, this is unexpected! Yes, Sir, I am. Training has only just begun, though…"

"No matter, I was hoping to receive regular updates from you throughout training anyway. This initiative is important to me, so I expect to be kept in the loop."

Bloody brilliant. If Oliver Teese had his way, she would end up reporting on Alpha Squad's failures to General Stone while telling Teese stories about how she was doing the best she could. What could possibly go wrong?

"Anything I can do to help, Sir."

"Wonderful. Why don't you tell me about your initial impressions of the recruits," Oliver Teese said.

Janine rested her head in her hand. This was not how she liked to conduct her training. At least military men like Stone had a solid understanding of the unwritten rules and boundaries.

"As I said, it's still early days. We have a lot of work to do just for assessment purposes. I would be more able to report on the trainees' performance at the end of the first phase of boot camp," she explained.

Oliver Teese sighed at the other end. He was obviously

not pleased with her answer.

"I don't need to remind you that you report to me now, do I? Alpha Squad was my project, and I intend to know what is going on with it."

Janine rolled her eyes. *His project.* "I understand, Sir. It's just that I have not even had the chance to individually assess each of the cadets yet. Reporting on their performance would be really premature."

"Fine. But I do hope I can count on you to check in as soon as you have something to of note to tell me, yes?" Teese insisted.

Janine ran her hand over her smoothly tied back hair. "Of course, Sir."

"All right then. I'll be waiting for your call." With that, Teese cut the connection.

At that very second, there was another knock on the door.

"Blackwood here. May I come in?" a voice asked.

"Just a moment," Janine responded, as she dialed Callahan's extension.

"Yes, Major?" the private answered.

"Could you get me a glass of water, please?" Janine put the phone down again and located Blackwood's grade sheet on her desk.

Between resisting her attraction to Eric and warding off intrusive questions from politicians, Alpha Squad was turning into an even bigger headache than foreseen. Not to mention that weird voice she'd heard.

And this was only day one.

CHAPTER SIX

Eric's heart sank when his one-to-one with the major ended. He did not want to leave her presence, but he had no other choice.

Hopefully, his answers had pleased her. The last thing he wanted was to disappoint this woman, even if he wasn't fully convinced of Alpha Squad's proposed relevance. Unfortunately, he had become so distracted looking at her that he'd found himself simply going through the motions during the whole assessment.

Had she felt it too?

Her bodily reactions suggested she was as attracted to him as he was to her; her elevated heartbeat, shallow breaths and dilated pupils were clear indicators. Still, the divide between them could not have been bigger. You did not date a recruit, obviously. It was unprofessional, and from the start, Eric had been able to tell that Major Williams took her work very seriously.

If only his inner bear could accept this fact.

Eric found himself lingering outside her office longer than appropriate. But the sound of her voice as she answered the phone kept him captivated.

Who was she talking to?

Oliver Teese.

She did not sound pleased. Sadly, Eric's hearing was

not powerful enough to be able to make out the exact words spoken by the man on the other end of the line. He would have loved an insight into the goings on at Alpha Squad and the challenges the major faced.

With every further answer the major gave, Eric could hear her tense up more. She was being cryptic on purpose, as anyone would be in her situation. Oliver Teese might have spearheaded the initiative to set up Alpha Squad, but it was inappropriate of him to expect to micro-manage it.

Eric's protective instincts kicked in. He felt for her. If only he could step in and make things easier somehow.

If indeed she felt the same as him, that very thing would probably make everything worse.

Perhaps once they completed their training…

Or if Oliver Teese lost interest in his little project after realizing that he wasn't going to have as much oversight as he expected, perhaps the whole thing would fizzle out and they could get on with their normal lives.

Perhaps then the two of them would have a real shot.

Eric forced himself to move when he heard approaching footsteps.

"I finished my lunch and just wanted to see how you were getting on," Blackwood remarked as he spied Eric in the hallway.

"My assessment has just finished. I'm sure you'll be up soon," Eric said.

The wolf nodded at him as he passed by and knocked

on the major's door.

Eric could just about make out the sound of the major's voice asking Blackwood to wait a moment, followed by a phone receiver being placed back in its cradle, as he walked back in the direction of the break room. Blackwood seemed nice enough, if a bit naive and overzealous. Hopefully he hadn't realized that Eric had been eavesdropping on the major.

Eric didn't have too much experience dealing with wolves, but he did know they were extremely loyal and could really hold a grudge. And if he took Blackwood's words at face value, the wolf's loyalties lay squarely with the squad and its leadership, not with any one of the individual recruits, least of all him, a bear.

"Please tell me there's food left," Eric remarked as he pushed the door to the small mess room open.

Adam grinned at him and held up a plate with a couple of fried eggs. "Obviously! But I don't think we can manage dinner with what we've been given."

Eric gladly accepted his share of the meal. "Perhaps we ought to do something about that, then."

Adam frowned. The two humans looked similarly puzzled.

"We're hunters by nature. Do I have to spell it out for you guys? If this training is all about us taking initiative, then we better get on with it."

Adam nodded slowly, but did not seem convinced. He was such a city bear! If they learned nothing else from this whole experience, at least Eric might end up taking his little brother out for a proper hunt in the wilderness. That had to count for something, right?

And if Blackwood was on board, they'd have half a chance of bringing home something worthwhile.

———◆———

When Cadet Blackwood entered, followed by Callahan with her glass of water, Janine still didn't feel quite right. Her earlier conversation with Eric King had affected her, mainly due to the voice in her head that she'd been unable to place.

It was like a second presence had infiltrated her mind, seeking to influence her and make her do things she'd regret.

The phone call with Secretary Teese had only made things worse. It had reminded her of just how much scrutiny she would be under. No matter what her *real* orders were, supposedly, she would have to answer for whatever happened with Alpha Squad. Teese would not let the task force go down as a failure, and General Stone would not allow it to succeed. A rock and a hard place. And on top of it all, a sexy bear shifter who kept looking at her like she was dessert.

Janine swallowed hard and looked up at the wide-eyed werewolf who stood in front of her desk. Out of everyone, Blackwood was by far the one with the best attitude throughout the morning. Was this guy for real? It was her duty to find out.

"Let's begin, shall we? Please sit down," she said, though her heart was not in it at all.

Blackwood nodded eagerly. "Yes, Ma'am."

She picked up the questionnaire and read out the first item. The same thing she had asked Eric only a short while earlier.

"Why join Alpha Squad?"

Janine did her best to listen to Blackwood's answers, taking notes whenever appropriate. But her mind kept wandering back to Eric King, comparing Blackwood to King in every possible way.

If this was how every assessment would go, she was doomed.

Still, she forced herself to continue and finish the questions.

After that, she instructed Callahan to hold off on sending any more recruits in. She needed a moment to compose herself.

Just as she leaned back in the squeaky chair behind her desk, the wretched phone rang again.

Now what?

"Yes, Callahan?" she answered, wearily.

"I know you did not want to be disturbed, but I have General Stone on the line."

Bloody hell!

"Put him through," Janine mumbled as she pinched the

bridge of her nose.

"Yes, Ma'am."

"Major Williams," the general addressed her.

"General. To what do I owe the pleasure of your phone call?" Janine tried not to sound sarcastic, even though *pleasure* was the last thing she felt right now.

"A status update. You might have formed some first impressions by now?"

Not this again!

"Sir, it really is rather early for that. I've only done the first two individual assessments so far." Janine tried her best to remain calm, but her heart was once again hammering away in her chest, and this time it was due to frustration, not lust.

"No matter. I mainly intended to confirm that we're on track," the general probed.

Janine shook her head. "I've prepared a standard boot camp training schedule for Phase One, Sir."

"And?"

"Physically, they're in decent shape, Sir."

"And mental assessments are not yet complete."

"No, Sir."

"I've had a word with Secretary Teese earlier today," the general said, pausing.

Perhaps that explained why Janine's phone had been ringing off the hook today.

"Yes, Sir?"

"We both agree that with a task force such as this, there is no need to hold back. He has approved my suggestion of incorporating a more rigorous course of training."

"Indeed, Sir?" They might have both agreed on something, but their motivations were the exact opposite.

"Once Phase One is complete, you are to incorporate aspects of Special Forces training into the syllabus."

"Yes, Sir." Janine made a note. Special Forces training. That was intense. "Any particular activities you propose, Sir?"

"Intense survival, advanced weapons, and parachute training."

The line went silent for a moment as Janine noted it all down. Why the hell would Alpha Squad members ever need to learn parachuting? The general was having a laugh, surely.

"You will be provided with the necessary equipment and be approved for use of the on base air strip by the end of next week."

"Thank you, Sir."

"Carry on. And don't forget your orders, Major." The general hung up and the line went dead.

Janine put the pen down and shook her head. Save for Bentley, none of the recruits were even remotely qualified for this.

The general would have sold his idea to Teese as a positive; Alpha Squad would be the most intensely trained domestic force of the country—provided the recruits successfully completed the course. Of course, the general's ulterior motives were still very much in play; he was simply setting everyone up to fail. Anyone with a shred of military experience could see right through this.

Of course, Janine did not have any choice but to obey, no matter how inappropriate the orders were. But she would not do so recklessly. Special Forces training was taxing and risky even for the most experienced and capable operatives. Lives were at stake.

A knock on the door interrupted Janine for the umpteenth time today.

"Who is it?" Janine asked, quickly closing the notes she had taken outlining General Stone's insane plan.

"Ma'am?" Private Callahan opened the door slightly and stuck her head in. "A quick moment, please, before the next assessment?"

Janine nodded at her and gestured at her to come in.

She closed the door carefully behind herself.

"Ma'am, I don't mean to be out of line…" she began.

"Speak freely, Private." Janine sighed and sat back. Nothing Callahan could say would make the day any worse than it already was.

"I couldn't help but overhear the conversation between General Stone and yourself."

Janine looked up and scrutinized Callahan's face. The woman looked skittish, as she usually did when faced with a superior, but that wasn't all. Her eyes were full of concern, perhaps even fear.

"Your thoughts?" Janine urged her to continue.

"Well, Ma'am, of course I don't have to tell you that Special Forces training is extremely demanding…"

"I'm fully aware."

"And the recruits are… well… for the most part not exactly…" She paused, as though she was looking to Janine for further reassurances.

"The recruits are not Special Forces material. Except for Bentley," Janine completed the private's thoughts.

Callahan nodded. "I was here last year when we lost two men to bad weather during SAS Selection training."

Janine folded her hands and stared down at them. This was exactly what had worried her too.

"I'm not looking to repeat that tragedy," Janine said.

"Indeed, Ma'am. I just don't think—"

Janine raised her right hand and nodded. "I understand and share your concerns. In fact, I have a few thoughts to minimize the risks."

Janine opened the folder in front of her and pulled out her notes. "Alpha Squad training Phase Two will be just a little bit different than your ordinary SAS Selection process. Especially for the purposes of extreme survival— arguably the most dangerous part of the training—we will not be sending the recruits out on their own."

Callahan raised her eyebrows. "No, Ma'am?"

Janine shook her head and a subtle smile formed on her lips. She wasn't sure exactly where the idea had come from, but it made perfect sense to her now.

"We will join them. If we are going to be a team going forward, we all have to play our part, don't you think?"

"Really?" Callahan's eyes widened further, until she caught herself. "I mean, yes Ma'am, whatever you say."

"What do you say, are you ready to participate in some advanced training?"

"But… This is quite irregular."

"Everything about this team is irregular," Janine remarked, mostly to herself.

She wasn't quite sure how far she was willing to take this, but this was the best way of making sure nobody came to harm. If Callahan and she accompanied the recruits on their exercises, they would be able to carry the necessary communications equipment enabling them to organize a rescue if things went south.

It was perfect.

Callahan blinked a few times, then she also smiled briefly. "Well, ever since the military has lifted its restrictions for women within the service, I have been wondering what it would be like to undergo rigorous training like that."

"I like how you think, Callahan. Glad you're on board. We will keep a close eye on everything from the inside and show the guys what we're made of as well."

Callahan nodded. "Yes, Ma'am!"

When Callahan left, Janine took a deep breath. Getting

closely involved in the advanced training was the only solution that made sense and would keep everyone off her back. Just because General Stone had come up with this ridiculous plan to sabotage Alpha Squad in its infancy did not mean she had to send her recruits into dangerous situations on their own. In the end, their safety was *her* responsibility, nobody else's.

CHAPTER SEVEN

The first two weeks of training went by in a whirlwind. They did everything Eric had expected to happen: cross-country runs, obstacles, problem solving, and hand-to-hand combat. They had even done some basic firearms safety. The shifters excelled at almost everything, but especially those tasks that relied on strength and endurance. Shooting, not so much, but that had only been a small part of their training.

As a result, the humans had exactly zero chance of coming out on top in the rankings.

The main reason why Eric and the other shifters felt worse for the wear was the unpredictable schedule, sleep disruption, and irregular meal timings. There was always something going on, the major made sure of that.

At the same time, Eric felt that she was purposefully keeping her distance from all the recruits, but especially him. The implied rejection, as much as he understood her likely reasoning, added yet another layer of mental strain to their already challenging situation. This was not how these things were meant to go. Both bears and wolves tended to have very simple relationships: once a potential partner was identified as a shifter's true mate, that was that. There was no denying it, no fighting it, and certainly no ignoring it. But she was a human, not a bear, so perhaps that stretched the rules a bit. Either way, Eric could not force her into acknowledging their connection if she did not want to.

The physical demands of the training were starting to take their toll on the humans as well, yet Bentley, the oldest of the group, seemed to revel in it. He was the only recruit who seemed to know exactly what was going on. His body clock had adjusted to the extent that he was already awake and organizing his uniform before the major came in to formally give them their orders each morning. Eric often found himself wondering if the man ever slept at all.

Most of the group was made up of strong, sometimes difficult personalities, meaning Bentley's assumed superiority had made him somewhat unpopular. The exception here was Blackwood, of course. The wolf was still frustratingly optimistic about everything, and seemed willing to accept orders no matter who uttered them. He was many things—fast, strong, ferocious when he wanted to be—but a natural born leader he was not. As the most easygoing of the team, he provided a bridge, a bit of cohesion between the humans and bears.

Meanwhile, Adam had taken on the role of cook, however grudgingly. Bears had a lot of strengths, but one of their weaknesses was their inability to function properly on an empty stomach. Plus, as Adam had remarked on their first day, he actually *had* relevant previous experience.

As a wolf, Blackwood was not as affected by their lack

of regular meals, but he'd eagerly volunteered to help them hunt when supplies went down. Together, they had managed to catch some small game and fish from the hilly nature reserve that surrounded Brecon, the town that was home to their base.

No matter how incompatible the group seemed, Eric had come around to Alpha Squad a little bit. The idea behind it was still nonsense of course, and the recruits were all inappropriate in their own way, himself included, but he had to admit that the experience was changing everyone little by little. His little brother had turned from unreliable and rebellious into somewhat of a team player in the span of almost two weeks.

Even Cooper, as stubborn as he was, had become just a little bit more respectful over time.

And Eric himself? He had actually started to feel like he belonged somewhere again, as stupid as it sounded. Ever since the New Alliance had become less relevant on-ground and more of a media sensation, he had missed the feeling of being a part of something bigger than just himself.

And so they all found themselves in the kitchen having a quick breakfast when the by now all too familiar sound of Callahan interrupted over the intercom.

"Cadets, the major expects everyone outside in five for an announcement."

Eric and Adam shared a look. Not an exercise, or a

drill, but an announcement?

"Don't just stand there looking like idiots. Hurry up!" Bentley barked from across the room and clapped his hands to make his point.

Eric glared at him. One of these days he'd punch the man and shut him up permanently.

Still, he was right. Eric finished his breakfast with one last bite and deposited his now empty plate on the table before heading out the door.

Everyone was outside much sooner than the five minute deadline announced by Private Callahan. The major was already waiting as well, clipboard in hand. How was it that she could look fresh at any time of day, when Eric himself so clearly felt the side effects of lack of sleep and a regular routine?

"Cadets," she started. "You'll remember I mentioned this training program had a number of different stages when you first arrived. Phase One is now over."

Eric exchanged a look with Adam and Blackwood, who stood toward either side of him. Then he stared at *her* again. The woman of his dreams. She was right there and yet they might as well be on opposite sides of the earth. It hurt, but he couldn't look away.

Why do you avoid me? Do you not realize we're meant for one another? Eric held his breath and tried to suppress these and many other, similar thoughts.

"I'd also said that only those who are worthy were to remain on the team." Major Williams paused for a moment, then raised the clipboard in front of her. "I'm pleased to announce that everyone is through to the next phase."

She looked up and made eye contact with each of the recruits, skipping Eric, much to his dismay.

Why do you torment me so?

"Good job, everyone. We will start Phase Two tomorrow. Prepare yourselves, because things get a lot more challenging from here."

Challenging would be an understatement, more like impossible, a strange voice spoke in Eric's head.

He frowned.

"Alpha Squad has received authorization from higher up for advanced military training."

Eric glanced across at Bentley, whose expression turned painfully smug. He was right in his element.

"Until now you've been pitched against each other, but going forward, it will be important to work together as a team," the major said.

Eric glanced back in her direction.

No matter what the orders are, we're in this together, the strange voice said.

These little glimpses, these shreds—they were in his head, but they weren't coming from him.

It's her! His inner bear insisted it was true, even if he couldn't quite believe it. That meant that it was confirmed. They truly *were* meant to be mates.

But just because he could hear her didn't mean she could hear him. She was human, after all.

Eric raised his hand.

She shot him a quick look. "Yes, Cadet King?"

His heart jumped as she said his name. "Exactly how advanced is this training going to be?"

Eric looked around at his team mates. Blackwood was grinning like an excited kid on Christmas morning, Adam had one eyebrow raised in surprise, and Cooper just looked scared. Meanwhile, Bentley simply rolled his eyes. His question seemed valid, though, even if nobody else had been willing to step up and ask it.

"We will start with an intense survival exercise." Despite answering *his* question, the major was still avoiding eye contact with him. "But you won't be going out there on your own. We are a team. And we will train as such."

Intense survival? Just exactly what was Alpha Squad's role going to be when all of this was over? Had his expectations been that off? Liaise with police in shifter related matters, he'd thought. Not exactly Special Forces stuff like Bentley would have done in the past.

If only we'd met under different circumstances, the strange voice said, sending his own thoughts into yet another tailspin. If only?

No, his inner bear was not willing to accept defeat just yet, even if the rest of him was mainly just exhausted. How long could he keep on fighting? How long would he hold out hope?

You're mine, even under these circumstances. You just don't know it yet, he thought.

Then he shook his head. What a mess.

"Now, I suggest you use your day off wisely, because we'll push out at the crack of dawn tomorrow. Dismissed!" She turned on her heel and headed back inside with Private Callahan following closely behind her.

"This is brilliant, isn't it?" Blackwood exclaimed. "We all made it!"

Bentley left without saying a word, leaving only Cooper and the three shifters.

"We made it through Phase One," Cooper remarked. "But who knows, with the extreme survival and all. I never signed up for this stuff!"

"We're a team. And shifters are especially good at survival stuff, even if I say so myself," Blackwood interjected.

Eric nodded and forced a smile. The wolf was right; they wouldn't let each other fail. Still, he did not feel like celebrating. All was again not as it seemed. He had a lot to think about, mostly regarding the thoughts in his head that hadn't belonged to him. What did it all mean?

The major had not even looked him in the eye once since his assessment on the first day of training. And his inner bear was not having any more of it. Something had to change or he would lose his mind, especially if they were going to spend more time together going forward.

And so, rather than stay back in the shared dorm with the rest of the guys, Eric decided he needed time alone to think.

"Today, I think I'll go out for a hunt by myself," he told Adam as they reached their bunks.

His brother simply shrugged. "If that's what you want. Though we'd all probably be better off if we took the day to relax."

No matter how glum Eric felt, Adam's remark made him smile anyway. What a difference a couple of weeks at boot camp had made.

"You're starting to sound like Mom," he teased.

Adam grinned too. "You think so, bro? Damn."

But a spot of motherly advice from the most unlikely person in the room wasn't enough to stop Eric. He collected his backpack and some warm gear and nodded a goodbye at his little brother. "I'll see you when I see you."

And with those words he was out the door and heading back down the same hallway they had all passed through earlier. He slowed instinctively as he neared the major's office.

There was a conversation going on inside her office. The major and Private Callahan were talking to one another. Although Eric did not wish to intrude, he could hear it so clearly it was impossible to ignore.

They did not sound happy. They were talking about orders, just like in the major's thoughts during the announcement. The name General Stone came up.

*What had she meant 'no matter what the orders are?'
What* were *her orders exactly?*

Eric shook his head. No, he would not do this again, lurk around the major's office, listening in on conversations, just waiting to be discovered by Blackwood, or worse, Bentley. Whatever it was, it was none of his business anyway. He was here as a lowly recruit. Even if he knew what she was dealing with, it wasn't like he could help her out.

Eric took a deep breath and marched onward, out of the building. He headed for the tree line of the nearby woods surrounding their compound and put his half empty backpack on the ground. Then he quickly undressed and kept his clothes away before allowing his true instincts to take over.

He was going for a run in the woods by himself not just because he was running away from something, strictly speaking. This was also the only way for Eric to really be himself.

To let his bear roam free and blow off steam would be the only way for him stay in control of his instincts and urges come morning.

Tomorrow they were going on a survival exercise together, all of the recruits as well as Callahan and, of course, the major. He could survive the wild, no problem, but how was he going to survive being so close to her without acting on his desires?

He had the whole day to try to run it off and he wouldn't waste another second of it.

As soon as he had fully shifted, he broke into a trot and headed deeper and deeper into the woods, slipping through a breach in the base's boundary fence on the way.

They had explored a lot of this area before—Adam, Blackwood and himself—and located the best hunting grounds as well as streams and lakes abundant with fish. But he was not heading anywhere in particular.

Today he had just one aim: to get as far away from the major as possible.

CHAPTER EIGHT

After the morning's announcement, Janine felt more conflicted than she had since the start of this assignment. Her orders were clear, and ordinarily she would have just kept her head down and followed them.

But this was different. She had joined the military to make a difference in her life, to *mean something* to her country.

And General Stone's orders to sabotage Alpha Squad's success did not seem to help her country, or anyone else. They were rooted in ego, not aimed to serve the greater good.

She had gotten to know her little team a bit over the past two weeks and started to become personally invested in their lives. Of course, she had felt just a bit more deeply for Eric King than the rest of them, something that had made it even more difficult to do her job properly. In fact, letting Alpha Squad fail and leaving all of this behind would actually make things easier for her in that respect, but that was hardly the point.

Even if only half of the recruits were here of their own free will, rather than simply being transferred from other agencies, Janine was certain that deep down they were hoping to make a difference too. You did not join Special Forces—in the case of Bentley—or even the Border

Agency, where Cooper had been transferred in from, without a sense of idealism. There were plenty of jobs out there that did not carry the same risks with them that law enforcement or the armed forces did, so it took a special sort of person to sign up for them.

Furthermore, the training and timed exercises they had done so far had shown that each and every one on the team was able and willing to learn and improve. And it was wrong to undermine that. No matter what the general wanted.

Janine thought about this as she found herself moping behind her desk with a cup of mediocre coffee in her hands. She looked up and noticed that Private Callahan was waiting in the doorway, her head cocked to the side as she was looking at her.

"Yes, Private?" Janine asked, folding her hands and straightening her shoulders to appear more confident than she felt.

"Ma'am, I had a thought," Callahan started.

Janine nodded at her to continue.

"What if, rather than leaving the cadets to their own devices tonight, we organize a dinner to celebrate? They've completed Phase One, after all."

Janine stared bleakly at Callahan. Celebrate what exactly? That they were working against all odds with little hope of success, no matter how hard they tried? That the highest-ranking military man in the vicinity had made it his mission to sabotage the team?

"And Ma'am, I know about General Stone," Callahan added in a low voice.

Janine frowned. "What exactly do you think you know, Private?" she demanded.

Callahan averted her gaze. "This is highly irregular," she mumbled.

Janine gestured at her to hurry up and speak already.

"Well, the general and I had worked together before, and he made some remarks when I arrived on base which contradicted our official mission here." She stared down at the floor in front of her. "I had to assume that he assigned you here because you and he were on the same page, which is why I never said anything, until…"

"Well… Then you understand why I'm not keen on celebrating the team just yet." Janine folded her hands and placed them on the desk in front of her.

"I hope you won't mind me saying this, but your heart is in the right place, Ma'am. And I understand how difficult the situation must be for you, but I just wanted you to know that I'm on your side."

"Are you, Callahan? Are you willing to disobey the general's orders for this team? Are you willing to risk your entire career for what was essentially supposed to be a PR stunt to boost some politician's popularity?"

"Respectfully, if you believed that, you wouldn't have thought of ways to help the recruits through the advanced training," Callahan said. "Your idea of accompanying them on their survival exercise goes above and beyond."

Janine sat back and stared at the private. Janine had thought her meek and eager to just keep her head down and follow orders, but this was a different side to her which she'd never seen before. She had only known Private Callahan for only two weeks, but time had a different meaning while on posting.

Janine wanted to take the private's words at face value. She wanted to trust her. Callahan had been the only person Janine had spent any meaningful amount of time with while on base, which she realized colored her perception. But if she could not trust someone, who had already taken the risk of expressing opinions which clashed with General Stone's orders, then who could she trust?

Plus, the situation they found themselves in was already impossible. What was the worst that would happen?

"Why?" Janine asked. "Why risk everything?"

The private shifted her weight from one foot to the other and stared at the ground again. "This might sound naive, but despite everything, I really do think this team could make a difference. The recruits have shown marked improvements over a very short time. With the right leadership and guidance, I believe everyone could end up working very well together."

Private Callahan made a good point. Just the fact that everyone had made it through the first phase of training spoke volumes. Had someone told her on the first day that everyone would make it, she would not have believed it.

Despite their differences and varying attitudes, everyone had really tried to make the best of their situation.

"I'll think about your idea—about a celebration—but now I really must be getting on with preparations for tomorrow's excursion. Dismissed."

The private nodded and saluted Janine before turning around and heading out the door.

Janine sat back again and folded her hands together behind her head and stared at the ceiling. She hadn't lied; she did have a lot of prep work to do, but she also needed to think.

Private Callahan had voiced exactly what Janine had been mulling over ever since the general had informed her about the advanced training. Some people spent their entire military careers doing as they were told without ever questioning a thing or feeling a shred of guilt. Janine had been one of them; but then again, she had never received orders that invited this kind of scrutiny.

The reasoning behind General Stone's orders made sense, for him. He did not appreciate some politician meddling in matters that were none of his concern.

Frankly, neither did Janine. But it didn't have to be that way, did it?

Sure, Alpha Squad had been Oliver Teese's idea, but he was not personally in charge of it; *she* was.

And although Stone would have put her name forward

as a suggestion to lead the task force, he did not have the authority to transfer her out again if she did not do what he wanted. Alpha Squad had been set up by a special mandate approved by parliament. It was the Ministry of Shifter Affairs that governed Alpha Squad, rather than the Ministry of Defence, which oversaw the military.

That made her position here rather unique.

This was a big decision, one which would affect her entire future. But perhaps it was best to look at the basics: her reasons for enlisting in the first place. Perhaps Private Callahan was right. If they pulled together, Alpha Squad could make a difference too, in an area which was completely underserved.

Fine. Janine picked up a blank sheet of paper and a pen and started to write out a To Do list to prepare for the upcoming survival exercise. Thanks to her chat with Callahan, she had all but made up her mind. If the general did not press her, she would keep her intentions under wraps for now until she was certain they really did have a shot at success. It all hinged on how the cadets would do in tomorrow's exercise.

Business as usual, then.

She picked up the receiver.

"Callahan. Please make arrangements for a little trip off base for dinner. It's only fair the recruits get a proper meal in them before what I have planned for the morning. Try 'The Badger and Snake' on the outskirts of Brecon."

"Yes Ma'am. I'll let everyone know."

The change would do everyone good. It wasn't just skill and persistence that made a team; morale was important, too. And it wasn't too unusual to do something like this during boot camp. General Stone—if he even came to know about it—would not question it at all.

Now when Janine got back to work, she caught a little smile on her face. She felt lighter somehow. Even the crappy coffee tasted just a bit better.

———◆———

By five-thirty, Janine had organized her desk, making sure not to leave her training prep lying about the place. Not that she expected anyone to come snoop around while they headed off base, but one could never be too careful.

As she left her office, Callahan was just passing by.

"I told everyone to get ready. They should be out any moment now," Callahan said.

The two women shared a quick look of understanding. "Very good. Is the Land Rover fueled up?" Janine asked.

"Yes, Ma'am."

Sure enough, multiple pairs of footsteps could be heard marching up the hallway. The men were ready.

Janine stepped out the front door, looking down at herself as she did so. Callahan would have told them to come in casuals, but she was still in uniform. Should she have changed?

She shook off the thought. On any other assignment

like this, she wouldn't have, so why consider it now? She wasn't trying to impress anyone, was she?

Janine waited with her arms folded in front of herself as the recruits joined her outside.

As everyone assembled in front of the unimpressive looking building, she noticed one glaring absence. Eric.

"Where's your brother?" she asked Adam King.

The bear shrugged. "I'm not sure, Ma'am. He said he was going to go hunt by himself, but he's not back yet."

Oh well. Janine was not sure how to feel about that. On the one hand, she was relieved to not have to deal with him in a more informal setting, but on the other…

"No matter. We're all off duty, so this dinner is not compulsory. We'll get something packed anyway so he doesn't miss out completely."

Adam nodded. "Yes, Ma'am."

"Ready, everyone?" Janine asked.

The group stood at attention. "Yes, Major!"

Janine could barely suppress a smile. They really had come a long way in just two weeks.

She opened the passenger door of the Land Rover and got inside, while Callahan, who had just finished locking the barracks, took a seat behind the wheel. The recruits all got in the back, save for Blackwood, who paused.

"Ma'am, if you don't mind, it's rather crowded in here," he said.

Janine rolled down her window and gave him a questioning look. "I'm afraid this is the only vehicle authorized to pass through the main gates at all hours. Taking your own car is not an option."

"I wasn't planning to take my car…" Blackwood longingly gazed in the direction of the woods near the track that led out of the compound. "If you let me know where everyone's headed, I could squeeze in a little run. I might come across Eric and bring him along with me."

Janine glanced back at the remaining three recruits in the back, then looked at Cadet Blackwood again. "There's a pub just outside the main gates toward Brecon Village which you would have passed on your way here. If you prefer to travel on foot, I don't see the harm."

Blackwood nodded and smiled. "Thank you, Ma'am."

"We'll see you there. Let's go," Janine said.

Callahan turned the key, and the Land Rover's engine roared to life.

The drive passed by fairly quickly; the beautiful views of the surrounding scenery kept Janine entertained throughout. Luckily, it was still light out.

When they reached the pub, Blackwood was already there, waiting by the door, but there was no sign of Eric.

They carried on without him; a couple of rounds of lager followed by a hearty meal more than made up for the lack of decent food on base. The biggest surprise throughout the evening was Bentley. One round down, and he was in his element. The man seemed to have an endless supply of battle stories which kept the group—

Callahan and Janine included—fully entertained.

All in all, the night was a big success, much more so than Janine had expected. Still, Janine could not help but feel a hint of melancholy about Eric's absence.

CHAPTER NINE

Phase Two started before dawn the next morning, just as the major had said.

None of the shifters, including Eric, were concerned. Even Adam, who had previously been most comfortable in the city, had gotten somewhat used to the great outdoors during the regular hunting trips they'd embarked on.

Bentley had woken everyone up at four, and they were already mostly packed up by the time the major appeared inside the dorm half an hour later.

"Morning, Cadets! This exercise is going to be an individual test as much as a team test. No man will be left behind, understood?" she said.

Eric stole a quick glance in her direction. Were they really going to go out there and rough it together? Part of him felt it was a dream come true, and perhaps a chance to get closer to her, while another part dreaded it. If she continued giving him the cold shoulder, then the entire experience would just be torturous.

"We push out in ten minutes," she added, then turned around and left.

One by one, the shifters and humans finished packing up their kits and left the dorm. Bentley had warned them the night before that each of their backpacks would weigh probably about as much as Private Callahan did, but that had not fazed the shifters on the team.

Eric watched as Cooper struggled with his bag, giving him a hand in lifting it on his back. If they had to, he was certain the shifters could carry everyone else's stuff as well as their own and still be quicker on their feet.

Once outside the barracks, Eric was surprised to see the major and Callahan with bags of their own. They weren't quite as large as the recruits', but they did not look light either. So she *had* meant it: they truly were going out there as a team.

They did not speak much as they squeezed into the back of the old Land Rover that belonged to the base. With two humans and three shifters filling the two benches lining the sides of the vehicle, there was very little legroom.

"We get off nearer the hills, and from there, we continue on foot," the major announced, then she nodded at Callahan to start the engine. The old vehicle coughed a couple of times before roaring to life.

Eric forced himself to look away from her and instead studied the backpack between his legs.

I need you, stop ignoring me, his inner bear insisted.

As soon as he completed the thought, he heard the major's heartbeat surge. Although she was in the front and he was in the back, they were closer to each other than they had been in over a week. He could feel the tension she must be feeling; he could catch a subtle change in her scent, even.

Eric stealthily glanced at Adam, and then at Blackwood, but neither showed any sign of having caught on to what was happening behind the scenes. The bond between Eric and the major was intensifying, no matter how hard she seemingly tried to fight it.

He closed his eyes and tried to remain calm, leaning against the cold backrest behind him. *Focus, dammit.*

Eric did his best to concentrate on the sounds and smells of the outside world passing them by as they drove through the base and further and further into unexplored territory. Finally, it was time to get off. It was easier to divert his attention away from the major's presence out in the fresh air.

"We hike up to the top of the highest hill in the area. You'll use your maps and compasses to plot the course," the major said as she waited with her arms folded in front of her. "Bear in mind this is a timed exercise, but you'll have to conserve your strength to be able to construct some kind of shelter once you reach the top. The weather in these hills could turn at any moment."

"Yes, Ma'am," the team responded, completely in sync.

Eric took one glance at the map, then another up the hill in front of them, and exchanged a look with his shifter team mates. This was going to be easy.

Bentley and Cooper, meanwhile, did their best to figure out which one was in fact the tallest hill, where they were currently, and what would be the easiest route up.

"We go east from here," Bentley ordered. "Then we head north-east until we reach the foot of that hill. That'll be the path of least resistance."

Eric shrugged and pointed ahead. "Or we could just go straight, since we're being timed and all."

The face of the hill in front of them was steep. That meant they would have to climb rather than hike up.

Eric and Bentley both looked at the major for a decision, who threw her arms up in defense. "I'm just an observer. You guys plot the course for us to follow."

Eric then exchanged a look with Bentley. "What's the time to beat? I'm assuming you've done this before."

The man's chest puffed up. "Of course the drop off was in a different location then, but these hikes are designed to take all day. Ten hours, forty minutes was my time."

Ten hours? No way was Eric intending for it to take that long. "Okay, but seeing as this is a team exercise as well, let's handle this as a team. The three of us—" Eric pointed at Adam and Blackwood. "We will use our talents to get everyone up there. You guys handle building everyone's shelter once we reach. Deal?"

Bentley's jaw visibly tensed up. "Whatever you say, mate. If you think your route is better, be my guest."

It would certainly be faster. Eric nodded. "Great. Bentley and Cooper, if you fashion yourself some climbing harnesses, and Blackwood, if you get up there and secure some guide lines… That would help everyone get up there quicker."

Bentley stared at Eric for a couple of seconds longer, but then he shrugged and did as asked. Within moments, everyone was doing something or other, not in competition for a change, but as a team. This trend continued throughout the day; the shifters, who were stronger and more skilled at climbing, forged ahead, making sure everyone's stuff made it up the mountain, and the humans followed, supported by rope harnesses.

Thanks to Eric's idea, they reached the top of the hill in a record-smashing six hours and twenty minutes, followed by a couple of excursions off course by the three shifters to fetch firewood and the necessary materials for their night shelter.

The still sun hung high in the sky when the shifters took some well-deserved rest and watched while the human team members performed their agreed upon tasks. They had their shelter built up and a roaring fire underway well before dusk started to set in.

"Good job, everyone," the major said, wiping a stray lock of hair out of her eye as she spoke. "This one is for the books. Excellent team work."

Although they had made it look easy, everyone was exhausted by the end of the day. Exhausted, but proud of their achievement. Thankfully, there was no need to hunt for food as they had been given basic food rations to carry within their kits.

If all that hadn't impressed the major, Eric wasn't sure what would.

———•◆•———

Their first day out in the wild had not gone how Janine had expected at all. They had made the climb uphill much faster than any team or individual soldier had done in the past. She had made sure to record everything properly, so that if questioned, she could back her reports up with evidence.

General Stone had not thought things through. He had ordered Special Forces style survival training because he expected Alpha Squad to fail. He had not taken into account that shifters possessed special strengths and skills which allowed them to ace tasks like this.

Not that he could have known, really. Shifters had only just revealed themselves a few months earlier, so their strengths and weaknesses were not widely known.

But Janine had seen up close what these men were capable of, and she could not help but feel proud.

This was her team, and ever since deciding to do everything in her power to ensure their success, she had fretted about how to get everyone through this particular exercise. As it turned out, the recruits had not needed her help as much as each other's. That was team work at its best.

Save for the previous evening, when she had taken everyone out for a team dinner, she had not had the chance to see the dynamics between the different recruits. It was obvious that some of the personalities clashed. Namely Bentley and the King brothers. With this much testosterone in such close quarters, that sort of thing was to be expected.

And although last night she'd been partially relieved to not have to deal with Eric, tonight, she did not have this luxury.

She and Private Callahan retreated into their own private tent, while the others shared a larger dorm tent.

"That went pretty well," Janine remarked as Callahan secured the front of their tent.

The latter nodded. "Much better than expected, Ma'am."

Janine nodded and leaned back against her backpack. They had managed a near impossible feat together, and it had been far from easy on them physically. Sure, the two women had carried less stuff with them, but they had still taxed their bodies. Come morning, it would become clear just how many aches and pains would result from today's efforts.

Despite her limbs growing heavier with each passing minute, Janine forced herself up. The chatter outside had died down, meaning the men had most likely retreated for the night, giving her the chance for a little private time outside.

"I'll be back shortly," she mumbled as she fumbled with the tent's opening and staggered out.

The sky was clear, which was unusual for this part of the world. Countless stars lit up the tent site and surrounding rocks and shrubbery. Janine would have to walk downhill a bit for cover.

She took a deep breath and wrapped her warm jacket around herself. It was only late September, but the nights were already chilly in these hills. With the help of the star and moon light, Janine found the most gradual path down into some larger shrubs about thirty or so feet away from the summit.

She did not waste time, and soon after started her climb back up. That was when it all went wrong. A loose rock escaped from underneath her foot and sent her sliding down the side of the hill. She let out a low whimper as her hip hit a sharp protrusion on the way, all the while flailing and reaching out for whatever vegetation she could find to stop her fall.

This seemed to go on forever, until finally, she stopped slipping. But it wasn't a small tree or shrub that had broken her momentum, it was a firm hand around her wrist.

Janine looked up and found a pair of familiar eyes staring down at her. Eric King.

How in the world had he come to her rescue so quickly? There had been no activity around the camp as far as Janine saw. Perhaps he had been out and about as well.

"Gotcha," he said. "Terrain's treacherous around these hills." He glanced up at the summit, which was a good hundred feet away now.

God, that voice. Janine did not say a word as he lifted her back onto her feet; she could not find the words. Of course, it was not just his voice, it was his whole being that had affected her so. After trying so hard to do the best job she could, no matter what the assignment, at this moment, she wanted nothing more than to throw it all away.

You're mine. The same low growl entered her mind. This was totally the wrong time for her overactive imagination to kick in.

Am I? Am I yours? she thought.

I knew that you were from the moment I first saw you.

Janine was frozen in place, communicating with whatever that voice was—a figment of her own imagination perhaps—when Eric's eyes began to glow in the dark. In this light, it should not have been possible to make out their color, but they had very clearly turned warm amber.

"How are you doing this?" she stammered.

"Wait, you can actually hear me?" he asked, looking about as shocked as she felt.

Janine opened her mouth to say something, then closed it again and frowned.

I don't understand. I have my orders. I have a job to do. Why are you in my head?

A smile broke through Eric's formerly serious expression. *Because I am meant to be in your head. For whatever reason, we are meant to be in each other's lives.*

Janine shook her head. *That does not make any sense. And anyway, I never knew shifters could read minds.*

We can't. Only when we find our true mate can we hear their thoughts, and they can hear ours.

That was too much. Janine freed her wrist from Eric's grasp and started to walk away, still shaking her head. She could not accept this.

"Thanks for saving me," she mumbled as she fought the pain resulting from her fall and marched back toward camp. "I need some time to think."

CHAPTER TEN

Ever since the first night of survival training, Eric had been even more conflicted than before. Touching *Janine's* wrist—after that little incident he found it hard to think of her in less personal terms—had revealed a lot more to him than he had let on.

Yes, it was confirmed now that despite being human, she heard him in his head too. What he had not told her since was that during that all too brief touch, he had somehow received a massive info dump of memories from her.

From the moment they first met, to her initial briefing with the general when she had arrived on base. Even the issues she'd had dealing with Oliver Teese, the politician.

Eric knew now what she had meant when she had first thought about her true orders. Eric knew that Alpha Squad was meant to fail.

And as disappointing as that realization had been, Janine still was his mate. He had nobody to turn to; he could not betray her trust. Her secrets were now his secrets.

Eric supposed it made sense. He himself had not believed in the cause at first, so why would the military? It was just disappointing, considering how everyone had given their all, and in the end, it would be for nothing. He could tell that Janine shared this disappointment.

Nobody, especially not someone as ambitious as her, enjoyed heading up a losing team. Not that anyone could guess any of these things by looking at her. She conducted herself as professionally as she had done from the start. After their first night in the wild, they had done an endurance march lasting a full day and almost a full night.

After that, they had been split into two teams to act out a rescue and extraction mission.

They had performed well and passed the survival stage of their training. Janine had told them as much. Everyone, even Bentley, looked pleased by the end of it all; tired, but satisfied.

Eric knew better, of course. For all the improvement their team had shown, what was the point of it all? He could understand Janine's dilemma all too well. If her orders were to let Alpha Squad fail, then what could any of them do about it? Nothing.

They were just cogs in a much bigger machine which someone else operated. Worse, that someone higher up could simply pull the plug if they wanted to. They were powerless.

After a couple of days of rest on base, the next stage of advanced training was the only one Eric had dreaded as soon as he'd found out about it. Parachute training.

A bout of bad weather had delayed their first jump by a day, but the extra theory lessons had not been able to endear Eric to the idea.

This was going to be infinitely more difficult than anything they had been through so far, and that was by design, as Eric had learned from Janine's memories. This was perhaps the last chance for the team to truly fail, if they did not get their nerves under control.

As the cargo plane took off, Eric and Adam stared at one another. This was well outside their comfort zone. The New Alliance didn't have any budget for airplanes, and the brothers had not traveled much outside the country either. This meant that right now was the first time they were going to be in the air.

Bentley, of course, looked smug. Cooper didn't seem too fazed, and Blackwood was excited as usual. After weeks of physical dominance by the two bear shifters and Blackwood, perhaps now the tables were going to be turned.

The demonstration and theoretical training they had undergone leading up to this point had explained exactly what they were supposed to do. But theory was a lot easier than practice.

The military plane had no windows, so Eric had no idea how far off the ground they were already. This was probably for the best.

Eric's ears popped a couple of times before the plane seemed to stabilize. He instinctively checked the straps on his parachute harness. They *had* calculated things properly, right? He could hardly believe that this little contraption would be able to hold him once the time came.

It's going to be fine, he said to himself.

The door leading to the cockpit opened and Janine appeared. Eric noticed she was wearing the same harness and backpack combo as everyone else.

They were *all* going to jump? The realization sent his imagination into overdrive. What if something went terribly wrong?

"Listen carefully. In a minute, I will open the hatch and we will jump out one by one. You will keep an eye on your meters and engage the parachute by pulling the strap, just like I demonstrated earlier. If you fail to do so, or something goes wrong with the main parachute, the backup will engage automatically. Understood?" Janine said.

What if the backup fails?

But Eric didn't say that out loud. Instead, he merely nodded.

"Yes Ma'am." Blackwood all but cheered.

Bentley nodded curtly as well. Of course, he already knew everything as usual.

"Then, when your parachute opens, you will navigate to the large X on the ground. Callahan is already waiting on ground, and I will meet you there as well."

Adam folded his arms and tried to look tough, but Eric could see in his eyes that his brother was scared. As was he. But his ego didn't allow to show it in front of Janine especially. Of course, if she was listening in on his thoughts now, she already knew…

He rested his hand on Adam's shoulder and stared straight ahead.

Janine walked up to the hatch and opened the levers, which seemed to groan in protest. As soon as she finished, the outside noise became deafening. It was like a hurricane passing by.

Bentley jumped up. "I'll go first," he shouted.

Janine pursed her lips and smiled, then she gestured at him to sit back down. "You're the most experienced one here. You'll go last."

As soon as she finished her order, she adjusted the strap of her helmet and stepped up to the exit.

Don't do it! Eric's inner bear screamed. But she seemed oblivious to his protests—or perhaps she just ignored them—and took the jump a split second later.

He jumped up and followed. No way was he going to sit around here wondering whether she had made it down in one piece. That was not how he functioned.

"Oi!" Adam shouted behind him. He shrugged it off.

With his woman hurtling toward the ground below, it was every man for himself right now.

Plus, he wouldn't have a hope in hell of ever impressing her if he didn't step up sand do the job. Eric paused for a moment at the door, but then threw himself headfirst into the noise. *All or nothing.*

The feeling of free-falling for what felt like an endless

thirty seconds was unlike anything Eric had felt before. He closed his eyes for a bit to get used to the sensation, but that did not help. There was no getting used to it. It was alien, terrifying and exhilarating at the same time.

He pulled the cord exactly when he was supposed to; the chute deployed and caught him with almighty jerk.

This had to be something of a record. Never before had he heard of any bear shifter jumping out of an airplane before. And today, provided he didn't chicken out, there would be two. And a wolf.

He looked down and saw the X Janine had referred to, and a chute, presumably hers, navigating right toward it. Up above, a couple of figures appeared at lightning speed; the others, whose chutes had not opened yet. One by one, they seemed to stop in mid-air as their backpacks released the carefully folded up lengths of fabric. It was mesmerizing to look at. They floated so elegantly, navigating left and right to get the hang of how things worked.

It was magical and exciting. He felt invincible.

Then, Eric noticed one obvious odd one out. One team member whose flightpath had no elegance or control to it, and who seemed to just spin around his own axis again and again.

Adam!

Eric's heartbeat went into a frenzy as he watched his little brother falling just a bit faster than the others, despite his chute being out. Something had gone very, very wrong.

As Adam came closer and closer to his altitude, Eric could see the problem. He wasn't in human form anymore. Great big furry paws tried to hold on to the reins of the parachute, but were unable to operate them with the finesse required to steer properly.

That was when it happened to Eric as well. He felt the change overcome him so quickly he could do nothing to stop it. His protective instincts had disabled his conscious decision making processes. His brother, his flesh and blood, was in trouble, and his bear reacted.

He tried his best to get close to Adam, but it was no use. There was no way he would be able to help him like this.

Eric closed his eyes and forced himself with all he had to push the bear back into its cage. *For Adam. Oh please, I can't let him down!*

It worked, just about. He found himself somewhere in a half state that at least allowed him to get closer to his brother.

"You've got to focus, Adam!" he tried to shout, but it sounded more like a growl.

"It's not working! I'm going to crash!" Adam screamed.

"Trust me. Shift back."

"How?"

"Don't argue. Just do it!" Eric urged.

"I'm going too fast!"

"Pull both the cords at the same time," Eric said,

remembering their briefing just before take-off.

Adam did so, clumsily, and sure enough, he slowed just a little bit.

Eric did his best to match his brother's speed, but he wasn't exactly an expert himself. Then, from the corner of his eye he spied Bentley, who started shouting instructions of his own. They could barely hear him over the sound of the passing air.

"Left!" Bentley seemed to say.

Adam turned his head, looking at the middle-aged human. "What?" he barked.

"Pull left!" Bentley repeated, louder this time.

Eric shook his head. "Shift back. You'll be able to do it if you shift back. Clear your mind."

It was Bentley's turn to look confused. The problem wasn't that Adam was unwilling to operate the chute properly, it was that he simply couldn't like this. It was hard to be delicate when you had paws the size of dinner plates.

"Clear your mind, dammit!" Eric shouted again.

Adam finally stopped flailing around and closed his eyes. The change was subtle at first, but when the fur started to vanish from his hands and arms, Eric could finally breathe a sigh of relief.

"Bloody hell, you were right, bro!" Adam shouted, when finally the chute reacted to his much more subtle inputs. "It's working!"

Eric exhaled sharply. He knew in his heart that a lot

could still go wrong. At least Adam was on the right track.

"Aim for the X," he said, and followed his own instructions.

It only took a few minutes for the bears to reach solid ground. They had landed surprisingly near the X, all things considered.

The major and private Callahan were already waiting.

That was too bloody close for comfort. Eric ran his hand through his hair and let out a nervous laugh.

Are you OK? Her voice, no, her presence, entered his mind, just like it had done up on the hill during the survival exercise.

Fine, but perhaps let's not do that again, he thought, then he diverted his attention back to Adam, who was still trembling, even though his feet were firmly planted on the ground now.

Eric scrutinized his brother's uniform, which was completely ruined and hanging off his now fully human body in tatters. That was when he noticed that Adam was looking back at him with an amused grin on his face.

"Made it. But I think we both need some new clothes."

Eric looked down only to find his own gear in much the same condition.

Then he looked up and saw that Callahan was stealing glances in his and Adam's direction. *Awkward.* Janine glanced up once before taking the clipboard from Callahan's outstretched hand and making a few notes. Had she taken a peek herself?

I'm so sorry, the same voice said.

He wasn't sure what she was sorry for, exactly, but at least he seemed to have gotten her attention again. His inner bear rejoiced at the thought of her checking him out, even if his human side still felt a bit embarrassed.

He hadn't shifted involuntarily like this in a very long time. In fact, not since that initial incident that had forced their family to move to East London when he had only just developed the ability to transform.

Perhaps now Janine would decide that she'd had enough time to think and let him get closer to her.

CHAPTER ELEVEN

That image.

No matter what Janine did or how much she tried to distract herself, that image of Eric post-shift was etched into her mind. What a sight he'd been. She'd sent him and his brother off to get changed, of course, as she waited for the rest of the team to land.

As it happened, she had done her best not to react openly; surely, the entire episode had been embarrassing enough as it was. Private Callahan had not been so subtle, though; as soon as the King brothers had made it to the ground and shifted back into their human form, her eyes had come close to popping out of her head.

They were beautiful men, so Janine could not blame her.

It had been a close call, though. Adam's jump had very nearly resulted in disaster.

When General Stone had ordered her to step up the training, she had never once considered that anything like this would happen. It occurred to her that there was a lot more to shifters that she didn't know anything about. She owed it to everyone on the team to find out.

Sadly, neither the military nor any other arm of the public sector had any guidance available on shifter behavior yet. Before they did anything else, she would have to devise some sort of training on these topics for Phase Three. Not just to educate herself and prevent any more accidents, but also to educate the human element of the team.

This was completely new to them all, but still she blamed herself for not realizing it sooner. As she'd watched the two men lose control in the air, one persistent thought had wormed its way into her mind and stuck there. *What if I lose him?*

Just thinking about the possibility hurt, like she would lose a part of herself in the process if anything happened to Eric. Not that that made any rational sense.

Then again, if anything happened to Eric's brother, or even anyone else on the team, she would never be able to forgive herself.

Perhaps in her feverish attempts to ignore Eric and maintain her professionalism, she had unfairly ignored the needs of the bear shifters. She had not allowed herself to be open to their concerns or understand the differences between them and the humans and endangered her recruits in the process.

No matter how confusing their exchange up on that hill during the survival training had been, she had to talk to him now. She had to involve the shifters more somehow, to prevent anything like this from happening again. Since Blackwood was too easygoing and Adam lacked relevant experience, Eric was the most logical choice to help her formulate a plan.

Could she trust him, though? She had felt him in her mind and gotten a feel for his intentions and his deepest desires. Her gut told her yes. Whether she could trust herself around him was a whole other matter, though.

Still, there had been no other incidents during their first jump, and even Adam and Eric had made it near enough the large X that she could tick this particular task off her training schedule. If anyone wanted a redo, that was up to them.

General Stone would not be pleased at these updates, but that was hardly her fault. Despite his best efforts, the team had made it through the most difficult parts of Phase Two and there was nothing he or anyone else could do about it.

———— ◆ ————

Janine barely knew what to do with herself when Eric entered her office. She had asked Callahan to summon him, determined to get some kind of shifter awareness training underway, but now that he was actually here…

The tension, the buzz in the air that separated them, was too much to bear.

I almost lost you today, Janine thought.

Eric smiled subtly. *Can't get rid of me that easily.*

She sighed and shook her head. If someone had told her three weeks ago that she would meet a guy whom she could telepathically communicate with, she would have feared for their mental wellbeing. And yet here she was. And more to the point, here *he* was.

She had hoped to keep this discussion professional, but with him in her head, that was beyond hope. Although he'd always respected her rank when speaking out loud, this more intimate version of him was unapologetically informal. And it did not even occur to her to correct him on that. In fact, she kind of liked it.

"I called you in here because…" The longer she looked at him, the more she found herself lost for words.

Because?

Why is it easier speaking to you like this rather than out loud? Janine wondered.

Now, what had just been a little smile playing on his lips turned into a full-blown grin.

Because you can't fight it any longer.

Janine folded her arms. He was right. She no longer even *wanted* to fight her feelings. But it was all so weird, so new to her, and she was unsure how to handle the situation.

Why didn't you say something sooner? Janine demanded.

Eric took a step in her direction, causing her to tense up and hold her breath again.

Would you have believed me if I had?

No, perhaps not. *Definitely* not.

"So what do we do now?" Janine wondered aloud.

Eric walked up to her in long strides until he stood just beside her chair. As she looked up, she was inexplicably drawn toward him. Before she knew it, she was standing right in front of the broad man who towered over her. How tall he was. And how incredibly sexy.

You tell me, he growled.

Janine closed her eyes and tried to concentrate, even if his musky cologne threatened to overwhelm her senses. Business first. She could not allow herself to get sidetracked now.

"The parachute incident."

Images of the aftermath of the incident, which had resulted in the two men landing in a state of undress which left very little to the imagination, flooded her mind.

Oh, is that what we're calling it? Eric teased.

"You and your brother almost got hurt. I can't have stuff like that happening again," Janine said, opening her eyes again in an attempt to get rid of her visions of Eric's naked body.

Just like that night out in the wild, his eyes developed a warm but noticeable amber glow. Yet another weird shifter thing she knew nothing about. How much else was there to find out?

"If Alpha Squad is going to be of any use, we need to know more about each other."

I'm all for learning more about you. Eric's eyes grew even more intense. It started to look like they were catching fire.

"I mean us humans. We need to know more about shifters. And vice versa."

Eric pressed his lips together, forcing his expression back to neutral and nodded. "Agreed."

God, having his voice in her head as well as hearing it out loud now fanned her desires even further. *Let's get this over with,* she thought.

"I want you to put together a training program for the rest of us to follow. Covering special abilities, strengths, weaknesses, traditions, whatever you can think of. This will be incorporated into Phase Three of training."

Eric nodded solemnly.

Thankfully, that was done. Then, without warning or sense, she felt herself tiptoe to get closer to Eric. Precisely at that time, he started to lean down and reach out for her face.

She closed her eyes and surrendered. To him. To her own desires.

Their lips connected and time seemed to stand still. It was the most beautiful thing. The firm grasp of his hand around the back of her neck paired with the almost careful, gentle dance their tongues started to perform. With every second that passed like this, their movements grew more deliberate and feverish. It was like this was only the first stage on a journey of pleasure and there was no stopping things before they escalated.

How she wanted this man. How she wished he would just take her across her desk and make her his.

Janine pulled back and shook her head. This was so unlike her. Allowing herself to be this vulnerable with a guy whom she arguably hardly knew. She'd had casual flings before; the army life basically meant that mostly there was no opportunity for anything more, but she'd never given up this much of herself before. Then again, this did not feel casual.

"Stop," she whispered.

Eric opened his eyes and let his hand slide down her shoulder before coming to a stop just above her elbow.

I can't do this. Not now. Not while we're still in training.

She studied his face for any sign of disappointment or anger, but there was none. He seemed relaxed. Though they did not glow anymore, his eyes were warm as they gazed down into hers.

I understand. At least you realize the truth now. I'll be waiting for when you're ready.

"Tomorrow we do some target practice, then Phase Two will be over. Phase Three is all about strategy and procedures. And whatever you come up with. I would love an overview of the topics you intend to cover on my desk by tomorrow evening." Janine averted her gaze for fear of losing control again.

He let go of her, causing her arm to almost ache at the absence of his touch. Janine listened to the sound of him walking away toward the door, yet she did not call him back as much as she wanted to. Their kiss had taken the edge off.

See you soon, she thought just as the door clicked back

into position, with him on the other side.

She needed to focus now and ensure that the rest of Alpha Squad's training passed without incident. So far, things had looked pretty good for the team. If they continued along this trajectory, nobody, not even the general, could declare the task force a failure.

Janine plopped down onto her chair and rested her head in her hands.

This was by far the craziest thing she'd ever done. Kissed a man at work. A recruit, even!

She should be ashamed of her lack of impulse control. She should…

But she wasn't. Although she could not let things continue just yet, their kiss had been the most glorious moment of her life so far.

Everything about it had felt right.

And for once, ever since coming to this base and starting this assignment, Janine did not feel alone anymore. They might not have discussed their relationship properly yet, but she knew it in her heart. He would be there for her, no matter what.

Funny, how after years of keeping a wall around her heart, it had taken a man from a whole other species to break through her defenses and show her hope. This assignment had been a struggle on so many levels; she had been asked to choose between the military and her conscience, her professional ethics and love. Finally, she could see that it was all completely worth it.

CHAPTER TWELVE

Eric was still reeling with the after effects of his encounter with Janine when he walked out of her office and through the hallway. Although his inner bear had tried its best to break free and take over, he was thrilled with how things had gone. Sure, she had cut their kiss short. Sure, he would have loved to see where things could have gone if she hadn't, but this was an epic breakthrough nonetheless.

She acknowledged their bond.

She felt as strongly connected to him as he felt to her.

There was a spring in his step as he headed back to the dorm, so much so that he caught himself and tried to tone it down as he entered. The last thing either of them needed was to draw attention to their budding relationship.

This was not the right time, he agreed with her on that. And if Alpha Squad was to fail anyway, they would find themselves in a much more favorable position soon enough. There was no need for her to get embroiled in a sex scandal with a recruit on top of everything else.

Possibly that was the reason she asked him to devise a training plan to educate the humans about shifter behavior as well. She was doing everything in her power to give the team the most comprehensive training possible so that she could not be personally blamed for its failure.

Of course, he would do his part, there was no question

about that. It was not her fault that those higher up opposed the idea of Alpha Squad. Though he did feel bad looking at Adam and Blackwood, who were still going through their respective parachute jumps blow by blow, just like they had done when Eric had been called away. Those two would take Alpha Squad's failure the hardest. They were the only ones here who'd actually volunteered. Bentley probably had his Special Forces career to go back to. And perhaps whatever Cooper did to earn him a transfer into this mess could get resolved if Alpha Squad was disbanded.

Of course, Eric had a future with Janine as his mate to look forward to. That was how shifter couples worked. Once you felt the true bond, there was no going back from it. And since Janine felt it as strongly as he did…

"Hey, bro. Everything all right?" Adam said.

Eric nodded. "Yeah, fine. The major wants me to prepare some additional training."

As soon as he mentioned the major, Bentley's head jerked up in his direction.

"Shifter related topics," Eric clarified and watched as Bentley looked away again. He must have been jealous that Janine had not involved him.

"Like what?" Blackwood asked.

"Basically she wants to know everything there is to know about shifters. Differences in behavior, etc."

"That makes sense," Cooper remarked from the other end of the dorm. "I don't know nothin' about shifters, except what I've seen from you lads."

Eric nodded as well. "Well, exactly. So we're going to rectify that."

Bentley let out a grunt and lay back on his bed with his arms behind his head. "Don't they have books about stuff like that?"

Eric decided to ignore him, but Blackwood eagerly stepped in to answer. "We've only just come out, as it were. Do you think we would have let people write books about us while we were doing everything possible to keep our existence secret?"

Bentley shrugged. "It's been a few months."

Adam straightened himself and joined in the argument. "Well, by all means, you head to the nearest library tomorrow and ask to see their shifter section. Let us know what you find."

Eric raised his hand. "Enough! Jan-the major asked for me to prepare a curriculum, so that's what I'm going to do. Only following orders."

Bentley did not respond, but his expression was dark as ever. After weeks of being Janine's second in command in certain exercises, clearly he was now jealous of Eric's assignment. *Who cares?* In a couple of weeks, none of this rivalry would matter anymore.

Eric sat down on his bed and grabbed a notepad and pen. If he wanted to have anything remotely close to a training plan by the following evening, he'd better get started.

——◆——

The following day's training had again seen the entire team perform well. The shifters were the weaker shooters, but they weren't bad at it. With enough practice, they would be able to catch up with Cooper and perhaps even Bentley.

It was strange to think that in another few weeks this was all meant to be over.

If the whole team continued to do as well as they had done today, how would they justify shutting it down? It was a mystery to Eric.

Despite these and other, much more intimate thoughts clouding his mind, he had still managed to complete his own assignment. He had penned an overview of training topics regarding shifter behavior for the humans, and even added any questions the shifters still had about human behavior. Even though Eric and his brother had lived in close proximity to humans all their lives, there were certain things that still confused them. These knowledge gaps were even wider in the case of Blackwood; wolves were notoriously clannish. He had grown up in a commune up in Scotland where no human had set foot in years and only headed out into the 'real world' a couple of years back.

So as soon as the target practice training had finished for the day, Eric headed to Janine's office armed with his notes and a pen, ready to report on his efforts so far. He instinctively slowed when he heard Janine's voice. This was becoming a habit: lurking around her office, trying to listen in on conversations. And a completely unnecessary one at that, now that she had come around to their relationship.

Eric knocked on the door to her office. *I'm here,* he thought.

Come in, she responded.

There. Much easier. She would have sensed him loitering out in the hall anyway.

Janine was still listening to someone on the other end of the line as she gestured at him to take a seat.

"I understand, Mr. Secretary. That will be very helpful," she said.

Teese? Eric guessed.

She nodded.

"Yes, we can begin next week. All right. Thank you so much, Sir. I'll keep you updated." Janine placed the phone back in the receiver and shot Eric a quick smile.

What a difference a few days had made. Eric was still getting used to this new and improved Janine; she was like an entirely different person.

What? Her voice infiltrated his mind again.

Nothing.

You're smiling.

Eric shook his head. She was right, of course, but it wasn't for any particular reason other than just being alone with her again.

"We'll be getting some police training next week," Janine said. "That's what Secretary Teese called me about. The Ministry has arranged for a qualified trainer to teach everyone about police procedures and relevant laws and regulations."

"I'm sure that will be helpful." *Even if the team is doomed anyway.*

Janine frowned. *What do you mean the team is doomed?*

Eric leaned forward and scrutinized her face. She looked concerned and he could sense a surge of anxiety originating from her.

Your orders. The general.

Then, she visibly relaxed a bit. *Oh, that. I'm still getting used to you poking around in my head like this.*

Vice versa, he responded. *So what's the story?*

Janine sat back and stared straight into his eyes. *General Stone, along with probably most high ranking officials from other agencies, have been unhappy about Alpha Squad's proposed role. They feel that the initiative should have never been approved.*

Eric nodded. That was understandable. They did not like another player coming in and stepping on their toes.

But we're not part of the military. Nor any other domestic force. We fall under the Ministry of Shifter Affairs and only Parliament can shut us back down.

A subtle smile broke through Janine's formerly stony expression. *As long as the team does well enough to satisfy Parliament and the Ministry, there is really nothing anyone can do.*

Of course, I was meant to stand by and watch as everyone failed the training, but they, I mean you, haven't failed.

What a relief. Eric had been dreading the thought of seeing his brother disappointed. This was the first time he had actually put his mind to something and followed through. Of course, it remained to be seen whether Adam would last once training was over, but just sticking it out here with all the challenges they had faced was a big deal.

The general must be pretty unhappy about that, Eric thought.

Janine's face and body language grew determined. *I imagine he will be furious, once he finds out. I haven't actually told him yet. I've been planning to wait until it will be too late for him to sabotage us.*

Eric nodded. *I'm with you, no matter what.*

Janine smiled again. *I don't know how, but I know.*

Eric leaned across her desk and took Janine's hand. She closed her eyes and sighed.

Ever since their first kiss, Eric had marveled at how different she was.

How tiny her hand felt in his. Her body seemed to be so much more fragile than the women of his species, but at the same time, she had a mental strength that continued to surprise him. She was willing to sacrifice her military career for this unit, even though she had been even less keen than him at the start of this assignment.

You believe we can do great things here, right? she asked, caressing the top of his hand with her finger.

Eric took a moment to think it through. He hadn't, at first. But as time had passed, he'd seen more and more potential and growth in the other team members. If he was in charge instead of Janine, he probably would end up doing the same thing.

There's a lot of potential here. I didn't think so at first, but now I've seen what we can do.

Janine smiled. *I'm glad we agree.*

"You have prepared a list of topics for Shifter Awareness Training?" Janine asked aloud.

Eric let go of her hand, unfolded the sheet of paper he had brought with him, and placed it on the table in front of her. She started to read, nodding and making little noises in agreement to various points he'd noted. It was the cutest thing to behold.

"That looks good. I'm looking forward to it," she said, looking up into his eyes again.

How he wanted to hold her again, kiss her again. He had always considered himself to be reasonably patient, but this was different. Now, he had all these urges and desires clawing at him that could not wait to break through his otherwise calm and composed exterior.

Especially since he knew she felt them too.

"I'd best be off then. Prepare more detailed materials," he forced himself to say.

Her eyes lingered on his lips for a moment.

I want to kiss you again.

Eric could not be sure if that was his thought or hers.

As difficult as it was, he shook it off. She had asked for time, to wait until their training was complete, and he would respect that. So he got up and started to walk away, even though his inner bear was roaring in anger.

Wait, Janine stopped him.

Eric turned to look at her. Her face was conflicted, as she got up from behind her desk with her hand resting on the surface. *Don't leave yet.*

It wouldn't take much. Just two, three steps to get to her position, gather her up in his arms, and satisfy all his deepest, most intimate desires.

I can't take it anymore. Is there somewhere private we can go?

Eric took a moment to clear his head, and then he had it. The perfect spot.

CHAPTER THIRTEEN

Janine did not know what had come over her when she asked to go somewhere private with Eric. It was so unlike her to change her mind once she'd made a decision. Then again, this entire situation with him was completely unlike anything she'd ever experienced before. She had hoped that their first kiss would reduce the tension, but it had just made her crave him more.

Janine watched as Eric stood at the doorway of her office and listened out for any sounds that suggested they might get caught. He gestured at her to join him. *All clear. Nobody's around.*

She just about remembered to grab her coat on the way out. Once outside the barracks, Janine felt Eric's eyes on her. *I could do it on foot, but a car would be better.*

She searched through the pockets of her coat, and luckily, there they were: the keys to the Land Rover. Janine tossed the bunch at him and approached the passenger side door.

It was already getting dark, making it hard for Janine to see their surroundings. Eric did not seem to have much trouble, so he scanned the area for onlookers one last time and then they were off.

At least now that they had taken the official base vehicle, Janine could explain their trip away as Alpha

Squad business. Something to do with the training Eric was developing for the team. Yes, that would be a decent excuse.

They did not speak as Eric drove along the bumpy tracks inside the base. Instead of turning toward the main gates, he switched off his headlights and took a left into some woods that were used for cross country runs.

Up ahead, up that little path, there's a log hut, Eric explained.

Janine squinted but could hardly make out what he was talking about. She could not see the track, never mind a cabin at the end of it. *How do you know?*

Adam, Blackwood, and I have had plenty of opportunity to explore this place. Where do you think we kept getting fresh meat and fish from?

Janine frowned. The rations provided by the base had mostly consisted of pantry staples along with a weekly delivery of fresh produce from the local village. *You guys have been hunting in these woods?*

Eric grinned at her. *Another thing I'll cover in Shifter Awareness Training. You humans would be surprised at how much food the average shifter goes through in a day. If we had not started supplementing our rations, we might have been tempted to eat the human recruits. Just kidding.*

"You should have said something," Janine protested. It was obvious she still had so much to learn. Good thing she had Eric as her ally now.

Eric chuckled. "It's been good fun, getting back to

nature like this after a lifetime in the city."

If after the rigorous training she had set up for them, the three shifters still had enough energy to go out and forage, perhaps she had been going too easy on them. Janine smiled to herself as she turned the door handle and stepped out. Now that the sun was down, there was a biting chill in the air that did its best to pass through her coat.

Eric joined her on her side and offered her an arm. "Straight ahead. We're not far off."

She took a deep breath, enjoying the prickle of the cold air against the inside of her nostrils. This place had its own beauty, even in the dark. The air smelled fresh, a bit damp, and laden with the heavy scent of pine sap from the surrounding trees.

She had not had much time to explore the base herself, which she now regretted. It was nice to get out of the cramped quarters inside the barracks.

Eric continued to guide her up a narrow track through the trees. Her footsteps seemed painfully loud against the near silent backdrop of the woods, while he was surprisingly light on his feet.

Eric was proven right, though. It took them hardly five minutes to reach a small clearing with a basic wooden structure in its center: the cabin he had been talking about.

Janine waited and watched as Eric opened the front door. It wasn't luxurious, but it could not have been more private.

He grabbed a candle and blew the dust off it before lighting it with a lighter he retrieved from his pocket. That gave Janine just enough light to be able to see the interior of the log hut better.

There was a fireplace, which Eric got to work on immediately, along with a cot in the corner that was covered with a formerly white sheet. Except for a couple of shelves, that was all the furniture there was. There weren't even any chairs.

While he managed to get a fire going, she uncovered the bed, dusting it off a bit. For a forgotten hut in the woods, it was not too bad. She had been made to stay in worse accommodations during previous deployments in her military career.

The previously lifeless pile of dry sticks in the fireplace started to crackle and pop as it caught fire, and Eric turned to face her.

She took a couple of steps back and sat down on the bed. The bit of padding provided by old blankets and things made it quite comfortable. She patted the empty space beside her and watched him as he joined her.

Ever since he had entered her mind for the first time, she had picked up on bits and pieces of his personality and character. She had *some* idea of who he was, but the gaps in her knowledge were huge.

I want to learn everything about you, she thought.

Eric leaned toward her and cupped her face again like

he had done just before that first kiss. She trembled and closed her eyes.

Me too.

When Eric's lips touched hers, he was filled with a fire even more intense than the one he had felt the first time around. Was it going to be like this each time? As far as he had heard, a couple's attraction, once mated, would never fade.

Shifters who were lucky enough to find their true mate would stay faithful their entire lives. *Till death do us part.* He pulled away to get a better look at her.

Janine's eyes opened and it was like he could see into the depths of her soul. This was the woman he wanted to spend the rest of his life with. He would take her back to meet his folks as soon as their schedules allowed. Once their situation here was a bit clearer, he wanted to make a home with her, perhaps even start a family, if that was possible.

His fingers trembled slightly as he traced the outlines of her face, down the sides of her neck, soon reaching the collar of her uniform. She continued to look at him throughout.

Is this okay? He pulled his eyebrows together, awaiting her response.

She simply reached for his shirt and pulled him closer,

lying down on her back as she did so. He did not need further prompting. His hands started their feverish struggle to rid her of her clothes as she started to fumble with his.

The small fire he had made had grown a bit and provided much needed warmth in the old wooden cabin. It was starting to get cozy. Not that they needed much outside warmth.

Her skin burned against his fingertips with a heat he had never come across before.

This wasn't his first time with a woman, and he imagined it wasn't her first time either. But it might as well have been—that was how different it felt. Her soft, pliable skin invited more detailed tactile explorations.

It hadn't taken long for both of them to find themselves completely naked. The rough fabric covering the mattress grazed his knees, but that did nothing to discourage him. Each time he looked at the woman below him, time seemed to stand still.

Nothing mattered anymore. Not her concerns about keeping things professional until the end of boot camp. Not even his worries that his work with the New Alliance had potentially made things worse. All they had been through had led them to this point. Now that they were truly together, they could take on the world.

"Kiss me," Janine moaned.

Eric muffled her demand with his lips, but she shook her head. *Not there.*

He covered her neck and shoulder in kisses until he reached the right spot. His lips and tongue teased and flicked at her nipples, first one, then the other, causing her to writhe against the bed.

This place wasn't perfect. The bed was not too comfortable for her either; he could sense it. But she showed no signs of regret, so he put his concerns aside and focused solely on giving her pleasure. The fact that they were finally together made everything more precious.

He slipped one of his hands between them, exploring the gentle curve of her side and her stomach, until he reached the soft mound of her sex. She leaned up and nibbled his neck, which sent shivers all the way down his back.

When the tip of his finger found its way in between her folds to her most sensitive spot, she cried out his name. Her already frantic heartbeat surged once again, almost matching his own. To his sensitive ears, it sounded like the beat of a drum, thumping faster and faster, setting the pace for their intimate dance.

"Don't tease me. I need you," she demanded, as she grabbed a handful of his hair.

He grinned down at her. Despite her much smaller size and more fragile physique, she had spirit, even in bed. *Your wish is my command.*

He had barely finished the thought before pushing her legs apart and getting in between, aiming his rock hard cock at her already moist entrance.

She bucked her hips upward, signaling that this was exactly what she wanted.

He did not wait any longer and entered her.

"Oh God yes!"

Her body invited him in, surrounding him like a soft but tight sheath. His mind grew cloudy; the details of their surroundings faded until it was all just a blur. The only thing in full focus was her. Her face, glistening slightly in the flickering light of the fire place. Reddened cheeks, feverish eyes. Her body worked with his in perfect harmony, thrusting and pulsating. Hips gyrating, muscles contracting.

Every move of theirs contributed to a shared goal. Pleasure.

He held on to her hips, raising her off the bed and onto his thighs. She reached out for his neck and lifted herself against him.

Now that they were sitting rather than lying down, she was in control. This was how she liked it, Eric could tell by her quickened breaths.

He held her in his arms as he continued to make love to her, faster and faster.

Little moans had escaped her lips when they just began, but by now they'd stretched and grown more intense. Luckily, the cabin was remote enough that they would not be overheard, not even by a shifter.

She started to shiver and tremble in his arms as he felt

her approaching climax. They were one now.

Her pleasure was his pleasure.

As the tension inside her grew, he found himself closer to the edge as well.

A pool of energy collected inside his core, pulsating in tune with their hearts, which had started beating in sync. With every thrust, it grew bigger and bigger until Eric felt ready to explode.

But it wasn't him who went off first. Janine shuddered against him and cried out his name again.

"Oh, Eric!" She dug her fingernails into his back, as though she did not mean for him to ever escape her grasp.

That sent him headfirst into his own orgasm. He grew rigid as his hot seed passed through his shaft and into her. It was a magnificent feeling, satisfying not just himself but his inner animal too.

He cradled her in his arms as they continued to sit up on the bed. Steam came off their naked bodies as they tried to catch their breaths.

After what felt like an eternity, he picked her up off his lap, allowing them both to lie down on the mattress. She had her eyes closed, though she was still awake. He listened to her slowing heartbeat and ran his fingers through her messy hair.

This was a sight he would not often get to see, especially not in front of others. Janine was always completely put together; he'd seen as much even the first time they met.

Neither of them spoke, aloud or even telepathically. They did not want to disturb the moment. And that was how they stayed for another ten minutes or so.

Their bubble of perfection burst much too soon as the sound of Janine's phone interrupted the silence. Eric could feel she was reluctant to let go of what they'd just experienced.

You'd better get that before people start to suspect something, he suggested, even though he felt the same.

She sighed and checked the caller ID.

"Shit, it's the general," she mumbled.

Eric kept as still as he could as she tapped the screen of her phone to answer. "Yes, sir?"

A gruff male voice spoke on the other end. He was loud enough for Eric to hear every word. "Major Williams. I was hoping for an update."

Janine closed her eyes and Eric wrapped his arm around her tightly. The call could not have come at a worse time.

"The cadets have completed Phase Two today," Janine said.

"Surely heads will roll now?" General Stone demanded.

"Actually, Sir, I must say they performed much better than we could have foreseen."

"Meaning?"

"They've all passed, Sir. They've made it to Phase Three."

Eric could hear Janine's heartbeat speed up again, though it seemed to sound different now that she was anxious rather than aroused.

"Don't tell me you've already announced their results?"

Janine glanced at Eric. *Well sort of, now I have.* "Yes, sir. It was self-evident. They know how they performed."

The general grumbled a few choice curse words on the other end. "And Phase Three?"

"Police procedures, laws, and regulations, sir. Secretary Teese has arranged for an expert."

"You had orders, dammit! Alpha Squad was not meant to succeed!" the general roared.

"Sir, we did the basic training and the advanced training, including survival and target practice. We even did parachute training just like instructed. They performed well against all odds. Every single one of them. If they are unable to pass the theory test at the end of Phase Three, that's a different matter, of course."

"Well. You'd better hope that they don't, Major," the general spat, then hung up.

I thought you weren't going to tell him yet? Eric wondered.

Janine closed her eyes and snuggled against Eric's still naked shoulder. *I've never been good at lying to people.*

Eric smiled. Fair enough, neither was he. *So we'd better make sure then that everyone does well during the coming weeks,* he thought.

Indeed. I'm relying on your help, Janine responded.

You can always rely on me.

CHAPTER FOURTEEN

Phase Three started with police procedures, courtesy of the expert instructor Secretary Teese had sent over. It was quite the learning curve, not just for the cadets, but for Janine as well, who sat in on the training.

If everything went according to plan, they'd be ready for action soon. And every single one of them, including Janine, needed to know how to handle the general public.

She found it difficult to concentrate; the memories of the night at the cabin had etched themselves into Janine's mind, making it hard to simply brush them aside. At the same time, Eric had taken on the role of star pupil; no matter what subject was being covered, he was ready to ask insightful questions.

As it turned out, there was quite a bit of overlap between the police training and his own shifter training topics.

Today's discussion: strength and abilities.

In a way, it was a relief for Janine to take a step back and let someone else take the lead on the training. The weeks that had passed so far had been stressful; they weren't an ordinary group of recruits, making their training even more challenging than a normal unit.

Of course, as Eric started to speak, Janine had trouble staying objective.

"Today Mike demonstrated some police techniques for restraining and subduing suspects. I hope you don't mind—" Eric glanced in the direction of the other man, who had stuck around to participate in Eric's session for the day too. "But a lot of these methods will not work for shifters. Here's why."

Eric waved Mike over. "Cuff me, if you please."

The hairs on the back of Janine's neck stood up. She had never known herself to have a dirty mind, but now, everything was different. She held her breath and tried to focus as Mike opened his handcuffs and approached Eric in much the same way he had taught the group earlier in the day.

But when he made a move to grab and twist Eric's arm behind his body, the maneuver failed. Eric's arm simply did not move, no matter how hard Mike struggled. It was obvious from his red and flustered complexion that he had put his all into the staged fight. Eric, meanwhile, had not broken a sweat as he stood his ground.

"You see, bear and wolf shifters possess the strength of about two to three human men, depending on their level of training. Female shifters are at least twice as strong as their human counterparts as well."

Mike stood back with his arms folded. "What's the solution? This sort of thing is going to become more and more important to regular law enforcement as well."

Janine looked around. Cadets Blackwood and Adam King seemed to have enjoyed the demonstration so far—

they were grinning like schoolboys—while Cooper's face could barely disguise the shock at what he'd seen. Not the brightest of the bunch, the former Border Agency man.

Even if Janine had not gotten to know Eric so intimately lately, she could have guessed at the shifters' superior strength. All the physical tests she had put them through during the first week of boot camp had shown her as much.

Eric straightened himself as he addressed the group, including Mike. "Well, it's all about finding weaknesses. Sometimes the only way to win would be to fight dirty."

The sound of a chair being pushed back made Janine turn to check the back of the group. Bentley had gotten up.

"Mind if I have a crack?" he asked, his chin jutting out in a show of confidence or arrogance, Janine could not be sure.

Eric raised an eyebrow. "Sure thing, mate. Do your worst."

Janine inhaled sharply. Things were about to get interesting.

Bentley approached Eric in a few long and resolute strides. Then he placed his hand on top of Eric's shoulder and grabbed his arm.

Eric let out a growl, but much to Janine's surprise, her man was forced onto his knees, with a triumphant Bentley beside him. The man had actually managed it. Eric glanced up and gave Janine a reassuring look. He was fine, even if he didn't look it.

"And that's how you do that," Bentley quipped. "Nerve points, lads! You'd be surprised how useful a little knowledge of anatomy can be."

"Right. That's what I was coming to," Eric confirmed as Bentley released him from his hold. He rubbed his shoulder and faced the group again.

"I've prepared a little diagram. Adam, if you could hand a copy to everyone." Eric gestured at the pile of papers on the table next to the wall. "Applying the right amount of pressure will give you an edge in hand-to-hand combat. Of course, this won't work if the shifter decides to change form, but it's better than nothing. I would also suggest the use of Tasers. We'll have to experiment a bit to figure out how many amps would be needed to effectively disable a transformed shifter."

Janine watched as Mike, the police trainer, took notes, and everyone else studied the diagrams. Funny, to think that the supposed expert sent in to train the team ended up learning a thing or two himself.

Eric's brother and Blackwood exchanged an apprehensive look. Janine supposed that they did not enjoy having their weaknesses exposed to the rest of the group, especially Bentley.

But if they were going to be effective at their jobs, this was exactly the kind of thing they needed to learn. With Bentley's and Mike's help, Eric demonstrated a few more moves that could effectively be used on shifters, then had Cooper repeat all of them once as well.

As soon as Cooper had managed to successfully copy even the final maneuver, Janine got up from her seat and nodded at Eric. "Good job, Cadet King. This has been extremely helpful."

You ain't seen nothing yet, Eric's voice spoke in her mind.

Perhaps you'll show me some more moves later, Janine teased.

"All right, I think this is enough for today," Eric addressed the whole group.

He had really taken to the role of trainer very well. It built on his strengths and experiences leading a New Alliance team. Janine suppressed a smile. She was lucky to have him on her side; actually, the entire squad was lucky. This right here was what would set them apart in the field.

Things were looking good. So long as nothing else went wrong, they would be unstoppable.

———◆———

The remaining weeks of training went by in a flash. Despite the general's warnings and threats, everyone, including the weakest of the group, Cooper, had passed the written examination conducted by Teese's expert police trainer, as well as any tasks Eric had set for Shifter Awareness Training. There had been no stopping the squad.

Janine's gamble of somewhat coming clean with

General Stone had paid off, so the invitation to today's ceremony would not have come as a complete shock to him.

The other thing that had paid off was her affair with Eric. Since that first night in the cabin, they had visited the place a few more times to spend more time together alone and get to know each other. So far, nobody had caught on, which was a relief.

Now, as she stood on the grounds outside their barracks in front of her team as well as the handful of other attendees representing the government, Janine could not feel anything other than proud. They had come so far in such a short period of time. Alpha Squad had made it against all odds.

Even the chilly October winds and onset of drizzle could not dampen her spirit.

General Stone, who stood toward the back of the group, glared at her, but his approval did not matter to her anymore. Despite everyone's differences and initial hiccups, the team had passed with flying colors. They were now ready for action.

"I'm not good at speeches, but I just wanted to tell everyone you've all done a great job," Janine began.

She scanned the crowd. All eyes were on her, but she remained unfazed and remembered the notes she had taken for today's occasion.

"In this past month and a half, we have come a long way." Janine looked at Eric in particular, then forced herself to pay attention to the others as well. "We all came from different professional backgrounds, carrying with us different sets of experiences and different strengths. But now, after the intense training we've been through, we have grown together, adapted, and learned more about each other. And though we started as a mere collection of individuals, we have now become a team."

Janine paused as she noticed Oliver Teese, fidgeting with a folded up piece of paper he had just retrieved from his inner coat pocket. Was he planning to make a speech next? *Typical politician.* She felt like rolling her eyes, but suppressed the urge.

"This unit is the very first of its kind, and that brings with it not just great responsibility, but also immense opportunity. We will be judged not just by the media and general public, but also by other agencies." Janine glanced over at General Stone, who looked even angrier.

"But I truly believe that we can do some good work together. We can make a difference. We are Alpha Squad!" Janine raised her voice to signal the end of her short speech.

The team, including Private Callahan, erupted in applause.

Remembering she had one more announcement to make, Janine raised her hand and everyone calmed down again.

"As a task force specifically devised to improve human

and shifter relations, I felt it only right that our command structure reflects that. I am therefore pleased to announce that going forward, Eric King will serve as my adviser in shifter related matters and right hand man, making him second in command."

Eric suppressed a smile as Adam and Blackwood came up to him, patting him on the back and congratulating him. Bentley, of course, looked least pleased of the group, but he would get over it. If Secretary Teese was to be believed, this would just be the beginning. Alpha Squad was just one unit now, but in time, that would change. Bentley would get a promotion in time, Janine would ensure it.

Janine saluted her team, a gesture which they reciprocated, and stepped away from the front of the crowd.

Oliver Teese came up to her and shook her hand. "Wonderful job, Major. I hope you don't mind if I say a few words?"

Janine forced a smile and nodded at him. "Of course not, Mr. Secretary." He could say whatever he wanted right now, as long as he did not meddle in the running of her team going forward.

As Janine joined her team and the politician started to speak, she saw from the corner of her eye that one very prominent guest had begun his departure.

General Stone, along with the commanding officer in charge of the Infantry School also situated on the base, had retreated back to their vehicle. She had not expected anything else from the man.

Janine had blatantly ignored his orders and there was nothing he could do about it. It was for the best. A man in his position was not used to having his authority questioned. No doubt he would be plotting some kind of revenge for Janine and the team, but that did not worry her. So long as the Ministry of Shifter Affairs backed Alpha Squad, he had little to no influence.

Oliver Teese's voice calling Janine's name brought her back to reality.

"…want to congratulate Major Williams on a job well done. And the rest of the squad, of course. We will do great things together."

Janine balked his last statement. *He wishes we'd be doing things together.*

That was when Janine felt a familiar pair of eyes on her from the other side of the little crowd.

He could be trouble, Eric's voice said.

I won't allow it, Janine responded. *Plus, he doesn't have operational control anyway.*

She could feel Eric smile, weird as that was. Ever since their first night together, their bond had deepened further. Janine could no longer imagine a life without him in her thoughts.

Once this little ceremony is over, perhaps we ought to get away for a bit… Eric suggested.

Janine's whole body grew a couple of degrees warmer at the thought. *I'd love nothing more.*

Although they'd only known each other for a month and a half—and during most of that time Janine had done her utmost to avoid Eric whenever possible—she had no doubt that their shared future was set.

She had never felt this way before; she had never been able to trust anyone else. Moving from foster home to foster home as a child had taught her to only rely on herself. But that was now over. The connection they shared ran so much deeper than any strictly human affair she had been involved in before.

Anyway, every relationship she'd had until now had been more casual than anything else. The intense demands of the army life had guaranteed that. But this, this was different, unique. They truly were one, with one common goal.

This was true love, even if so far it had felt too weird for Janine to say that out loud.

I love you too, she heard him say in her thoughts, and did her best not to blush.

EPILOGUE

It had been almost a week since Alpha Squad's official graduation ceremony. They were a proper task force now, no matter how much General Stone hated it.

Despite that, they were still lingering around on this base where they had spent the last month and a half, waiting for further orders. It was fine and well that all the recruits had made it through Boot Camp, but without being deployed anywhere, Alpha Squad might as well have failed just like Stone wanted. Plus, it would only be a matter of time before he would try to make their life here miserable. He had no influence over the squad directly, but the entire base itself fell under his command, and as such, he controlled their infrastructure.

Janine sat at her desk, shuffling around paperwork. The grade sheets and training schedules were ripe to be filed away until a later date when someone new would join their ranks. But she was only half thinking about the future of the task force. There was another, more pressing matter on her mind.

Eric.

She had always vowed to keep her professional life and personal life separate. Fate had intervened and forced her to reconsider.

But this was not the military anymore, this was Alpha

Squad. That meant it was a new job, with new expectations and new rules.

And after everything they'd gone through together, she knew that she could not have done it on her own.

Eric was her right hand man now, a position which extended into her personal life as well.

Of course, that was no reason to rub it in people's faces either. Bentley had wanted a more prominent role in the Squad, so any hint of impropriety in Janine's choice would get him even more riled up.

No, they could not openly celebrate their love; at least, not yet. But that did not make what they had any less special to Janine. This was the first time she had ever felt so deeply for someone else, after all.

The phone rang—a sound that had previously only ever meant more complications—but on this bright young morning, Janine did not mind.

"Yes?"

"Major Williams, I have Oliver Teese on the line," Callahan said.

Rather than dread the upcoming conversation, Janine was simply curious. Did he have some good news for once?

"Put him through… Yes, Mr. Teese. What can I do for you?"

"Major. I hope your men are ready?"

Janine's heartbeat surged at Secretary Teese's question. *Ready for what?*

"They are indeed, Sir," she said.

"Wonderful. We have a developing situation in Sevenoaks, Kent. One that might benefit from your team's special skills and expertise."

Janine pulled her notepad closer to herself and picked up a pen.

"No problem. We will be there."

"That's good to hear. My associate will stay on the line with all the details. A good day to you, Major."

"Good day, Sir."

Janine was still scribbling down instructions when the door opened and Eric appeared in her office.

Good news? he asked.

She smiled briefly. *We have an assignment.*

He approached her desk, leaned across it, and cupped her face in his right hand. *Great. When do we leave?*

Janine checked the clock on the far wall of her office. Sevenoaks would be a good four to five hours away by road, depending on traffic conditions.

"How quickly do you think the rest of the team could get geared up?" Janine asked.

A little glint appeared in Eric's eyes. *In about as much time as it would take for you and me to spend a bit of quality alone time together.*

Janine did not directly respond to him. Instead, she picked up the phone on her desk.

"Private. Get the men ready to move in an hour. We

have an assignment." She hung up as soon as Callahan acknowledged her orders. Then she diverted her attention back to Eric.

Well, what are we waiting for then?

- THE END -

ABOUT THE AUTHOR

Dear Reader,

Thanks for reading Alpha Squad: Boot Camp. This is the first book in my brand new Alpha Squad series, which serves as a spin-off to my well received Scottish Werebears series, which came out in 2015-2016. If you enjoy Vampire Romances as well, you might also want to check out my Vampires of London series in which I currently have three titles out; Alexander's Blood Bride, Michael's Soul Mate and Lucille's Valentine.

I may have only released my first book in 2015, but I'm not new to writing in general. In fact, my mom still tells me to this day about how I would make up stories, and attempt to record them in my clumsy, shaky handwriting from the moment I learned to read and write. From there I went on to write fan fiction and other stuff meant for my own eyes only.

I've always enjoyed stories of the paranormal. Vampires, shape shifters, witches and magic, all featured in the books I loved the most, even when I was still growing up. But it wasn't until much later that I got into romance. One of the first writers (a self-published author just like me!) I came across was Tina Folsom, via her Scanguards Vampire series. I was hooked. From there I went on to read more paranormal romance until I found a new kind of hero I loved: bear shifters, like the kind written by Milly Taiden, Zoe Chant, and T.S. Joyce. What I love about bears is how they can be all strong and independent, a bit reclusive, and almost grumpy, but they always end up having a heart of gold (plus they tend to know their food, and we all know that a man who can cook is doubly sexy). All that (except for the shifting into a powerful bear) almost exactly describes the sort of man I ended up falling for and marrying in real life, so it's no surprise that this is what I started my publishing career with.

To find out more, check:

LoreleiMoone.com (And why not sign up for the newsletter to be the first to find out about new releases.)

You can also get in touch with me via Facebook (search for Lorelei Moone), or email at info@loreleimoone.com

x Lorelei

BUT WAIT, THERE'S MORE!

2017 is set to be the year of Alpha Squad. In all, the series is going to comprise of four titles, three of which are releasing in 2017.

Alpha Squad Books:
Boot Camp (Dec 2016)
Friends & Foes (Apr 2017)
Infiltrator (May 2017)
Show Down (Jun/Jul 2017)

Eventually the whole series will also be made available in audio format, and an omnibus containing all four parts will be published too.

Alpha Squad has received its very first assignment and bear shifter Adam King is excited to jump head-first into the action. Upon investigating a string of seemingly shifter related murders, he finds himself torn between his job and the local police's main suspect; Felicity Weir; female bear shifter and Adam's fated mate...

Find out more about where to buy this book at loreleimoone.com.

HAVE YOU MET THE SCOTTISH WEREBEARS?

Before there was Alpha Squad, there were the Scottish Werebears… And if you sign up for Lorelei Moone's mailing list at loreleimoone.com, you get Book 1, Scottish Werebear: An Unexpected Affair absolutely free!

Titles in the Scottish Werebears series include:

An Unexpected Affair

A Dangerous Business

A Forbidden Love

A New Beginning

A Painful Dilemma

A Second Chance

These individual books in the Scottish Werebears series are best read in order. They can also be enjoyed as part of the Scottish Werebear: Complete Collection boxed set.

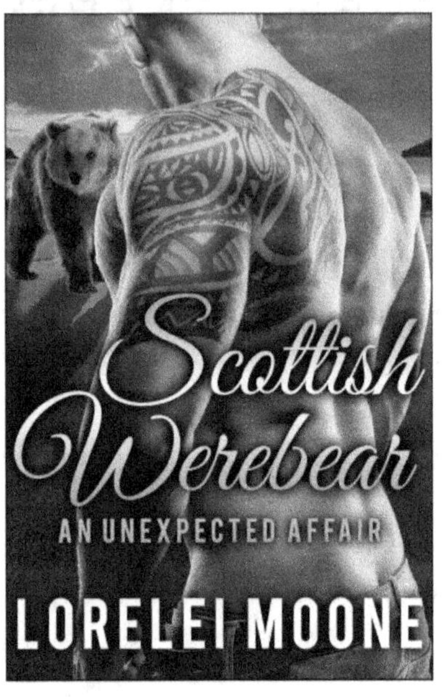

When romance novelist, Clarice Adler, hides herself away in a secluded holiday cottage to finish a book, the last thing she needs is another relationship. Imagine her surprise when she falls head over heels for the man who runs the place. Derek McMillan knows Clarice is his mate, but he's a bear shifter and she's human and the two simply don't mix. They are literally worlds apart; can they find a way to come together?

Get this book for free by joining Lorelei Moone's mailing list at loreleimoone.com!

www.ingramcontent.com/pod-product-compliance
Lightning Source LLC
Chambersburg PA
CBHW071016180726
48291CB00004B/1490